Capel Sion

CARADOC EVANS' NEW BOOK

CAPEL SION

BY

CARADOC EVANS

Author of " MY PEOPLE"

Another contribution to the complete study of the Welsh peasantry with which Mr. Evans made such a brilliant beginning in " My People." This book settles the anxious question of the author's staying power. Not one of the chapters is below the level of his former book; in the publishers' opinion a few are actually higher than his first amazing performance.

Front cover of the first edition (Melrose, 1916)

Capel Sion
Caradoc Evans

Introduced by
John Harris

seren

Seren is the book imprint of
Poetry Wales Press Ltd
Nolton Street, Bridgend, Wales
www.seren-books.com

© The Estate of Caradoc Evans, 2002
Introduction © John Harris, 2002
First published in 1916
This edition published in 2002

ISBN 1-85411-308-9

A CIP record for this title is available from
the British Library

*The publisher works with the financial assistance of the
Arts Council of Wales*

Printed in Plantin by
Bell & Bain, Glasgow

CONTENTS

INTRODUCTION

THE CARADOC EVANS we recognise first announced himself well in advance of *My People:* on 24 January 1913 to be precise, in a letter to the *Daily Express* printed under the heading, 'In Darkest Wales: Politics Masquerading as Religion'.[1] Signed David Caradoc Evans, the letter made plain that here was an insider speaking, 'a Welsh-speaking Welshman cradled in Welsh Nonconformity' who wished to report on 'my people'. And his message was that Wales was in a moral darkness because of religious tyranny:

> At every turn the Welsh peasantry are bled for funds to provide their pastors with salaries and to throw up unwanted chapels. In 99 cases out of every hundred the preacher is the wealthiest man in the community.
> And yet there never has been a creature who holds himself more aloof from his flock than the pastor. He visits the poor and the aged when in need of funds; never else.

In literature, drama and art, Wales lagged behind other countries because 'All along the line Welsh Nonconformity has sternly vetoed everything in the nature of artistic enterprise.' Furthermore, in a country in the grip of a priest-caste, religion functioned as the tool of politics; Sunday after Sunday congregations were hectored by ministers ('messengers of darkness ... wordy and frothy') whose instruction was, 'Vote for my man or you will be eternally damned.' Evans's compatriots were hard materialists; they lacked ideals and any freedom or independence of thought: which is why his letter, published as the Welsh Church Bill laboured its way through Parliament, welcomed the prospect of disestablishment. The Mother

Church had missed her mission in Wales; disestablished and reawakened, she would mount a challenge to Nonconformity, and so help rekindle the spiritual life of the nation.

Readers of the Conservative *Daily Express* would have been surprised to learn that Evans was a *Sunday Companion* sub-editor, a chapel-going Congregationalist well to the Left politically. Born on New Year's Eve 1878, and raised by his young widowed mother on a ten-acre smallholding in south Cardiganshire, he was put to drapery on reaching his fourteenth birthday. For the next dozen years he flattered and fawned behind shop counters in south Wales and London; as he reflected, 'I never exercised my brain, nor was I asked to exercise my brain.' His escape came after evening classes in English at the Workingmen's College, St Pancras, and through a chance opening in popular journalism, the field for self-made men and women in which he quickly prospered. By late 1913 he had left Northcliffe's *Sunday Companion* for Edward Hulton's penny weekly *Ideas,* a 'home journal' now totally forgotten but edited by Edgar Wallace at the time that Evans joined it and boasting a circulation of over two hundred thousand. In February 1915 the editorship passed to Caradoc, a post he occupied for the next two-and-a-half years, perhaps the most productive of his entire career. One contributor, the romantic novelist Edith Nepean, drew a picture of the 'wild Welsh editor chained up' in his den off Fleet Street: 'a tall dark-haired, dark-eyed man, wearing a coat with fringed sleeves and with a black cat in his arms'. The year was 1917 and the thirty-eight-year-old journalist something of a minor celebrity on account of a short-story collection which had become a literary sensation.

The circumstances of Evans's background most bearing on his development as author are by now well known.[2] He believed that Wales had been failed by her writers, both in English and Welsh, since nothing in their pages, in 'the pretty-pretty novels that are dear to my race', accorded with his experience of Rhydlewis; of being 'brought up amongst grinding poverty, always with the background of sanctimonious hymn-singing and hypocrisy'. That experience, painful and disturbing, he had absorbed and analysed over the years, and his letter to the *Daily Express* gave the essence of his understanding. It is no coincidence that he seriously took up writing later in 1913; he now had something to say, and the courage and confidence to say it. What he needed was a powerful medium to serve his precise intentions. He found it, appropriately enough, in the Bible and its way with story-telling; its language provided the basis for his own narrative prose: a strong, incisive instrument driven by anger and disgust yet remaining austerely impersonal, and with that quality of 'simple grandeur' he admired in the English Bible. Set within this narrative medium was a daringly-fashioned dialogue, designed to reveal the consciousness of his characters and the value system in which they are trapped. Truly original, in language as in subject matter (and Evans came to English with none of the proprieties of a native speaker), the fifteen stories published as *My People* (November 1915) showed just how potent, how weighty, the short-story collection could be, particularly where the component pieces share a single geographical setting and are further bound together by character, action and theme: by a coherent view of society, that is. *My People* in the context of Wales was an act of cultural terrorism, assailing popular notions of the Welsh as predominantly classless, living under enlightened leadership in some kind of Holy Land. Praise by English reviewers fuelled Welsh hatred of the book – as did Evans's high sense of mission: something soon apparent in the correspondence columns of the *Western Mail* where, with prophet-like fervour, he confronted his critics on the social message of his art.

'Naturally I want justice for myself and my book', he declared as *My People* faced charges of obscenity, 'but a much more vital issue is involved ... the undoubted right of the critic to pass judgement on the manners and customs of his time.' That time, we might remind ourselves, was a time of war, and the writer who was also an editor had a pulpit and platform from which to pass judgement on the moral life of both England and Wales. To an extent the war divided him: like every popular newspaper, *Ideas* could be counted pro-war – and Evans took particular pride in its circulation among the troops – yet until his dismissal as editor (in the summer of 1917) the paper maintained a strenuously radical position, thundering against the professional defenders of God, King and Country, and leaving readers in no doubt that besides the war against the Germans a civil war was being fought. The notion that in a period of emergency social divisions were being swept away Evans dismissed as fantasy; the truth was that they were intensifying. It is noticeable how fiercely he saw the war in terms of class conflict and economic injustice: week after week his column excoriated the likes of munitions magnates, government officials, food suppliers and profiteering tradesmen; week after week it headlined cases of working-class exploitation in the name of the war – munitions workers handling poisonous chemicals on a 'monstrously inadequate' six shillings a week; Belfast women weaving aeroplane linen for 'starvation wages' (3d an hour). Closer to home, he unequivocally defended strike action by Welsh colliers, even as others impugned their patriotism ('Germany's allies in Wales'); and his support continued when the men and their wives agitated for fairer government control of the milk supply. Here too were grounds for optimism, for 'when the South Wales miners set themselves a task they go through with it' (3 November 1916). But, as Evans explained elsewhere (*New Witness*, 7 December 1916), this Welsh coalfield militancy had a deeper cultural significance. In standing up to the coal owners the miners were at last breaking free of the chapels:

> No one can accuse the religious leaders of the Rhondda Valley of aiding and abetting the miners to strike. Most of the chapels are erected with the money of coal capitalists and upholstered with grocery, leather and drapery money. The men in the pulpits are the paid servants of their employers, and often the paid agents of Liberal politicians. 'Respect your rich betters' seems to be the motto of the coalfield preacher.

Besides the coal owners, another privileged group was profiting from the war. Why were the farmers so reactionary? *Ideas* asked. They greedily pushed up prices, treated farm workers like slaves, exploited child labour, and swindled the Exchequer out of millions in unpaid taxes. For the situation in Wales, Evans turned to an old school friend employed on the *Carmarthen Journal*. D. L. Evans's damning reports spoke of wasted acres that could largely solve the food problem were it not for the indolence of farmers and the shortage of suitable labour. Agricultural labour was scarce because Welsh farmers had never learned how to treat their workers as human beings (they were now abusing industrial English schoolboys). Meanwhile, they wallowed in excessive prices (for butter especially) and openly expressed the wish that the war would continue until they were wealthy enough to retire. Military conscription barely touched them, since they used 'all manner of dodges and backstairs influence to keep their burly sons at home to assist them in swelling their bank balance with blood money' (27 October 1916).

In truth this was not surprising. 'In all wars the idealist fights for an imagined golden land, while the practical man gathers a golden harvest at home', concluded Evans, for whom the Great War, far from destroying any meliorist illusions – those Enlightenment ideals of progress and man's perfectibility – was expressive of something absolutely native to our human makeup.

> We shall never have universal peace. At what time we shall not be fighting against a foreign enemy, we shall be fighting against our brothers and neighbours. Men will not cease to covet that which is not theirs, howsoever loudly they will cry forth their honesty. The humble shall serve the boastful; the rich shall be as gods, and they shall do no wrong, for the laws will be in their keeping.
>
> (6 April 1917)

The war reinforced Evans's convictions and deepened his creativity. Between April 1915 and March 1918 he published three dozen stories, many in the *English Review*, the most advanced of the literary journals (an outlet for Conrad and Lawrence), and some in Cecil Chesterton's *New Witness,* a serious left-leaning weekly strong on political corruption, 'the Achilles heel of Liberalism'. Between them they printed six of the fifteen stories that went to make up *Capel Sion,* Evans's second collection. All date from 1916, the blackest year of the war, one which began with compulsory conscription (Evans was exempted on grounds of occupation) and ended with Asquith's fall as Prime Minister – between came the carnage of the Western Front culminating in the Somme offensive. Though set in a pre-war period, *Capel Sion* tones with a contemporary reality in its depiction of a warring unto death over land and money, the protagonists intimate enemies who babble of god and religion.

For Evans's villagers are tethered to the chapel, all captives in a Nonconformist compound which is also a prison of the mind, erected over generations by preachers and Liberal politicians. Their god is the god of Sion, or more immediately, the Big Man's son on earth. To the Ruler of the Pulpit they make their sacrifices, for he is the community's protector – 'Your horses will rot and a plague of worms will eat your sheep. Lightning will burn your bellies and crops ... What will you do without me?' – and the arbiter of individual lives. Insistently Evans portrays debased religion as a weapon of social control, used to bludgeon, disgrace and humiliate, and always in the service of the powerful, the monied farmers chosen to be chapel deacons. The minister calls them blessed, and their prosperity is a sign of God's favour: witness Amos Penparc, 'whose riches were above any other man on the floor of Sion, and whose piety was established' ('The Pillars of Sion'); or Griffi Wernddu, 'cheapened in the eyes of Sion' by his material fall; 'none bid him to pray or to bear testimony in the Seiet; and to another was given his place in the Big Seat and also his office' ('A Sacrifice Unto Sion'). No nonsense here about rich men and eyes of needles, or of the meek inheriting the earth.

The Revd Davydd Bern-Davydd makes his entrance by way of a sermon on the widow of Nain, a biblical story exemplifying Christ's compassion for the poor but, in Bern-Davydd's hands, one more means of ensuring that even the 'religious little widow' gives of her mite. 'The Word' amusingly suggests how the chapel shapes community thinking; social distinctions are reinforced, as is the crucial identification of wealth and status with individual moral worth. Sion's ruler retains the outward attributes he manifested in *My People:* the lordliness, the vanity, the easy familiarity with the Almighty (to whom he is still 'Bern bach'), the theatricality and ready emotionalism so beloved of his congregation ('to weep to the tune of the Respected gives religious delight'). Nor has his verbal zest deserted him: 'The Comforter' finds him in full spate, no less comically deceiving at the burial of his wife. Evans palpably relishes his creation, at once a serious target and the source of comic grotesquery. 'The Word' even tempts the author into a few personal asides: Hawen, the Rhydlewis Congregationalist chapel he attended with his mother, is mentioned by name, while Evans's contempt for a tyrannical local schoolmaster fuels Bern's comment on Abed: 'his thick lips are gaped like the lips of the Schoolin when he desires Ellen Felin'. Caradoc himself appears under his local nickname: 'Shall that be said of you, Dai Lanlas, after the report that Eynon Daviss made about you?' asks Bern. 'A dirty black you was, man, to jeer at Capel Sion.' (The Revd Eynon Davies led the Welsh charge against *My People*.) Bern meets some improbable challengers, notably Dan Groesfford, the club-footed farm labourer who breaks his hire to answer the call of the ministry ('The Acts of Dan'). He has the cant, the empty eloquence, essential for pulpit success and, most importantly, some money at his disposal. Its source is Sali Blaenpant, the enigmatic 'stranger woman' who arrives unannounced at the village in her horse-drawn cart. Bern scents danger – and opportunity.

'Grasping is the Ruler of the Pulpit. Always asking he is, Pedr bach, for yellow money. There's a boy he is for his pocket.' The words are Pedr's, the half-mad would-be prophet who descends from the moor to preach the sins of Sion ('Calvary'); as in *My People*, he is ribbed and humoured until his truths become too barbed. But he knows Bern's essence, his need to exploit every turn of event for his own material gain. Others take their cue from the master. 'All for me, and the rest for my brother' is the sum of their ethical code – except that precious little brotherly love is in evidence. Indeed, the family remains the site of savage conflict, both between and within generations. (What family feeling there is resides in the doting regard of mothers for their ungrateful inadequate sons – the religious charlatan Dan sends his 'Satan of a Mam' to the local Poorhouse.) As ever in Caradoc Evans, men and women are brutally opposed, with men overwhelmingly the oppressors: Esther Crooked Tygwyn is a startling exception ('The Widow's Mite'), although mothers might inflict upon their daughters-in-law the wrongs they themselves have endured. Sion's males exhibit a puritan horror of sex. Periodically stormed by lust, 'My flesh is clean' they proclaim; and when events tell unambiguously against them, the chapel is ever at hand to assure them that they 'fell by an old female'. Whatever the imbalance of power, women are always the initiators, 'Satan's daughters' who break down their menfolk's defences then oppress them with the burden of their sin.

Such is Hannah Harelip ('Redemption'), a farm servant made pregnant by her employer Evan Rhos, which is an inconvenience for Evan as he closes in on a wealthy wife and decidedly troublesome when Hannah threatens him with the law. It is a futile gesture, as Evans's narrator makes plain: 'Hannah was told that it is against God's will for a servant to charge her master, that God does not permit them who sit in the loft of Sion to murmur against them who sit on the floor and in the high places'. Ellen Pugh is another made pregnant by a praying man ('A Mighty Man in Sion'), though here the forces are more evenly matched: Ellen at twenty-six is 'strong and ... proud of her chastity' whereas Lias Carpenter is a hollow Sionite propped up by his minister. He dries his trousers before Ellen's fire, and at the unignorable outcome furiously turns against her. Ellen determines to fight back, but can she survive without Sion when the Chapel is law and life? If servant girls are fair sexual prey, women of means are wife-material, to be snared for their money and set to work on the farm. Evans is eloquent on the fate of such women, 'crushed to the glazen dullness of cows by submissive giving, child-bearing, and continuous toil'. Thus Betti, wife of Griffi Wernddu, who bore eight children and 'laboured until the members of her body were without feeling' ('A Sacrifice Unto Sion'); or the dying Leisa, her marriage one long vicious sham, struggling 'to trim the land which gave her little and robbed her of herself' ('A Keeper of the Doors'). Both have husbands lost to religion, a condition not unfamiliar to the superintendent of the Carmarthen Joint Lunatic Asylum ('religious emotion ... is more apt to cause mental breakdown, and more apt to tinge mental disorder than other factors', he reported in 1905). Money worship, not a discomforting eschatology, drives Dennis Glasgoed insane ('The Tree of Knowledge'). His fevered imaginings coalesce around a supposedly wasteful wife and her likely collusion with his enemies. 'Sorrowful is this. All are in array against me.' And all must be made to pay.

Two stories featuring Amos Penparc form a continuous narrative ('Sons of Their Father' and 'Judges'), while Amos's rivalry with John Tyhen takes in 'The Day of Judgment', an uncollected story of 1917 written as a sequel to 'Judges' (and here printed in an appendix). These three related pieces might well be fragments of the novel which, towards the end of 1915, Evans was reported as writing: he had provisionally entitled it 'The Children of Essec' – which is what indeed are Amos, Daniel, Ruth and John Tyhen ('the child of his wanton days'). 'Sons of Their Father' finds them at the dying Essec's bedside seeking word of their inheritance. Amos stands apart, choosing to speak religiously, but 'an awful stealer is Amos', as John Tyhen rightly divines. The later stories have the two confronting each other over the meadow, Amos supported – outwardly – by his minister. John's resistance is stubborn and savage but the chapel breaks him down; he acknowledges Bern-Davydd's dominion; he comes to love Big Brother. Interestingly, the minister in *Capel Sion* regularly outwits his deacons whereas in *My People* it is (we sense) the deacons who ultimately wield the power. This said, 'The Pillars of Sion' shows Amos as a monster of evil, planning the seduction of the mentally disabled Silah Penlon. Here is a classic Evans configuration: a chapel elder in alliance with his minister bending a superstitious flock, and an outcast female reduced to animal status. Once again a widow is reviled, a frightened mother fighting to resist the community's view of her daughter ('mad bitch', 'the Big Man's curse'), and it is tempting to suppose that driving this staggering story must be Evans's feelings for his own widowed mother and her youngest son, his brother Josi. Severely handicapped, mentally and physically, Josi remained a helpless creature, his condition viewed in some quarters as a judgement on his father's dissolute life. (Repeatedly in this collection disability and illness are seen by Sionites as marks of God's disfavour.)

Though published on the heels of *My People*, and thereafter overshadowed by that (in)famous collection, *Capel Sion* has its own distinction. It is a darker, more claustrophobic collection. We rarely move beyond the unnamed village (recognisably *My People*'s 'Manteg'), which is itself less broadly realised: the working world rarely breaks in and the natural world is mostly present in the animal curses flung between the characters. These characters are fewer in number, with schoolteacher, shopkeeper and craftsman, the reprobates and the gossips, reduced to walk-on parts (the absence of children almost goes without saying: Welsh childhood-and-country heaven was a state unknown to this author). More telling is the lack of positive female presences, those resourceful younger women, shrewd, robust, intuitive, and aware of their physical attraction, who offer in *My People* some challenge to the men. Ellen ('A Mighty Man in Sion'), Ann ('The Deliverer') and Sali ('The Acts of Dan') touch upon on the type but, while marked off from the menfolk, they are diminished as agents of change. The reduced social canvas throws Bern-Davydd into relief; he and the workings of the chapel remain the focus of the collection.

Capel Sion quietly advances Evans's literary methods – a stricter authorial reticence, a more prominent Sionite narrator – and takes greater risks with dialogue (occasionally to the point of self-parody: 'Three Men From Horeb' buckles under the weight of mannerism). Yet mostly *Capel Sion* carries that sense of perfection deriving from Evans's genius for fashioning stories that completely embody his themes. Objective commentary and extraneous description alike become unnecessary; what we need to know about the characters we learn from their own words and actions. This was the first rule of his art – 'A novelist should neither praise nor blame. That's the preacher's job. His job is to tell the story.' To the American critic H.L. Mencken, this absence of praise and blame was the Caradoc Evans hallmark, and one which meant that his characters, repellent though they might be, were depicted from a viewpoint of no superior scorn or indignation; 'Somehow, Evans gets into his portraits a sense of their helplessness.'[3] This was surely his intention; however bleak the vision, there is compassion for the most defenceless and an understanding of others, the 'half-slaves, half-tyrants' whose tragedy is their helplessness and hopelessness. 'As they were born; so will they live. They are the victims of a base religion. They have been whipped into something more destructive than unbelief.'

For this second collection the publisher Andrew Melrose built upon a marketing strategy already in place for his author. He was the Welsh Zola, and the book a valuable social document, 'Another contribution to the complete study of the Welsh peasantry with which Mr Evans made such a brilliant beginning in "My People"', as the *Capel Sion* dust jacket put it. The accompanying photograph, of a sternly resolute Evans, projects a public image of the author in the wake of *My People* (see frontispiece to this present edition). The Evans-Melrose relationship warrants a moment's attention since it was no small risk for a publisher to take on this author in the first place: short stories were notoriously bad sellers and a first collection by a little known name bordered on commercial suicide. Furthermore, publishers were excessively nervous of any material that might possibly give offence; their timidity, more than the law, cramped artistic expression at this time. Yet Melrose had one advantage when considering Evans's work: he recognised its kinship with another book he would come to publish, *The House with Green Shutters*, George Douglas Brown's response to the picture-postcard view of rural society associated with Scottish Kailyard fiction. He and Brown had been close companions, sharing similar views on literature: 'There can be real literature that is without essential religion,' wrote Melrose, a Scottish Presbyterian with a background in the Sunday School League; and (Brown to Melrose), 'The damning fault of most of the books I read is that nothing in them seems to leap at you from out of the pages. They are talky-talky, vapid ... but most books of the kind we want, should be pregnant and packed.' When Evans offered Melrose exactly such a book, he saw it as a counterblast to the new Welsh species of Kailyard represented by Allen Raine, whose idylls of country life, set in Evans's very own Cardiganshire, enjoyed an international readership. Likewise Melrose accepted the author's reforming intentions; as Evans explained:

> Welsh novelists have in the past written stories which would have applied equally well to any part of the world if the geographical names had been altered. I myself wish to interpret the national life from within, to hold the mirror up to my countrymen and by displaying their weaknesses do something to stimulate the great revitalisation for which all patriotic Welshmen are looking.

Publication was justified on grounds of the book's sincerity: 'if you get sincerity and style you get literature at its best', remarked Melrose of Evans, and though momentarily unsettled by *Capel Sion* ('his new book is uglier than his last physically & I am secretly saying "no more"'), he stood by his man, for *Capel Sion* and *My Neighbours* (1920), and once again for *Taffy* (1924).

Capel Sion went on sale on or around 16 December 1916 to a predictable critical reception: what the *English Review* considered high art, the *Welsh Outlook* thought 'the literature of the sewer'. Apropos reaction in Wales, Melrose privately remarked how Evans seemed disappointed that his book had not been seized by the Cardiff police. The *Western Mail* did not disappoint, upbraiding an author who, having lived in a 'moral sewer', used his talent 'to bespatter his own countrymen with filth'. Evans responded with characteristic bravura. *Capel Sion* was more or less a true record of what he had seen and heard and experienced:

> In my youthful days West Wales was 'a moral sewer'. As it was, so it is even unto this day. The creed preached from the pulpit is that God can be hoodwinked and cheated, provided you do not cease in your offerings to the pulpit. The widow can be robbed, and the righteous mocked and driven to death. The man in the pulpit is King, and his orderings are as wicked as the orderings of the King of Prussia. It were better if on the site of every chapel in West Wales were erected a cinema palace.

Evans rode oceans of abuse – the critical hysteria energised him – but one accusation he could not let pass. Calmly and insistently, he rejected the charge that his stories were 'gross in tone, in content and in effect', as the *Western Mail* had claimed. 'Nothing I have ever written is gross in intention. No English reviewer, and I have been reviewed by many, has charged me with that offence, and it is significant that the charge should have come from Wales.' (In fact, a similar accusation surfaced in England in 1925, when Archibald Henderson's *Table-Talk of G.B.S.* classed *My People* and Lawrence's *The Rainbow* as 'pornographic novels'. Evans straightaway began libel action, winning £100 from Shaw in an out-of-court settlement.)[4]

As books change their meaning with their readers, so the timing of a book's publication can affect the way it is read. 'Patriotism was the temper of the time', recalled the poet A.G. Prys-Jones (then a musketry instructor at Dulwich College); and 'when thousands of Welshmen were dying abroad, one only felt contempt and loathing towards an author who denigrated his kinsfolk'. More precisely, Evans struck at the very moment Welsh national pride reached a peak, one week after Lloyd George became prime minister, he having ousted Asquith over the conduct of the war. (Asquith, laying down *Capel Sion*, is supposed to have remarked, 'And I believe every word of it'; the collection, we know, sent Margot Asquith 'into raptures').[5] These were heady times for the Welsh, as Evans acidly recognised: 'We hate the English as one hates a fool. God made him our servant and for one glorious period appointed Mr Lloyd George to govern this foolish tribe.'

Away from Wales, reviewers favoured readings that universalized the book's concerns: Evans was lashing the vices of a soulless Puritanism (with such bearing upon evangelical America that Mencken professed himself willing to donate a hundred copies to the YMCA). His art was obviously a selective one; however grounded in local incident, *Capel Sion* could not be thought to present a rounded social picture. Hannen Swaffer – quoting H. G. Wells's opinion of Caradoc Evans as 'a very fine artist' – pressed the author on the sources of his stories and was given examples of the kind of departure from fact (*Weekly Dispatch*, 14 December 1916). 'Redemption' recounted an actual happening, 'except that the girl refused to be enticed over the well'; 'The Widow's Mite' was 'true concerning the woman and the man. The cow is an invention'; and 'The Deliverer' accorded with the facts except – this a revealing deviation – 'that the woman [Ann] did not die ... In real life the woman, recovering, became a perfect vixen.' 'I have not written a word that is not true', concluded Evans, without making plain, as elsewhere he had been at pains to do, that fiction must always be 'built on the foundation of the author's imagination'. From the very beginning Evans dealt freely in fantasy, creating a personal imaginative universe from his own deepest experience and awareness of the world: it preserves the potency of his stories, which time has not dissolved. That certain events never happened did not make them less true; 'you know incidents more remorselessly true than anything I have written about in my stories', he taunted his critics. And such incidents have recently surfaced in studies of nineteenth-century rural Wales, more particularly those concerning the treatment of women and the exploitation of the agricultural poor. So much more 'remorselessly true' do they appear that Evans can now 'seem guilty not so much of malice as of understating his case'.[6] Reading a story such as 'Redemption' with a knowledge of the horrendous sexual abuse suffered by female servants on west Wales farms (and their total lack of redress in law) surely compels admiration for Caradoc Evans as a courageous reporter on conditions in his homeland. Andrew Melrose was right: the books *did* have value as social documents. Yet wasn't there another side to the picture? 'Oh yes,' Evans answered his publisher, 'but it is the ugly side of Welsh peasant life that I know most about'. There were many truths about Wales, but only one could he make believable. 'I like stories that are gloomy, morose and bitter', he confessed before a writers' circle; they answered his sense of the world as a place of ineradicable conflict and injustice; a world which while professing to value human charity, humility, sincerity and compassion actually rewarded the cruel and the overbearing, the avaricious and self-righteous. It was a disturbing vision, and one which he was repeatedly urged to soften. In time, in part, he would do so, but not in 1916; to quote Pound in one of his letters, 'If the poets don't make certain horrors appear horrible who will?'

JOHN HARRIS

Notes

[1] It was reprinted in the *Welshman* [Carmarthen], 31 January 1913, and in the *Glamorgan Free Press*, 26 September 1913. I am grateful to Dr Christopher M. Baggs for first bringing this letter to my notice.

[2] For an outline see 'Caradoc Evans, 1878-1945: A Biographical Introduction', in *Fury Never Leaves Us: A Miscellany of Caradoc Evans*, ed. John Harris (Bridgend, Seren, 1985), 9-45.

[3] From Mencken's review of *Capel Sion*, *Smart Set*, December 1918, 143.

[4] Shaw accepted responsibility for the text, for which he had passed proof, and paid a further £20 for a 'dignified apology' in the newspapers.

[5] Daphne Bennett, Margot: *A Life of the Countess of Oxford and Asquith* (London, Arena, 1986), 290.

[6] David Pretty, *The Rural Revolt That Failed: Farm Workers' Trade Unions in Wales, 1889-1950* (Cardiff, University of Wales Press, 1989), 213; see also Jill Barber, '"Stolen goods": the sexual harassment of female servants in west Wales during the nineteenth century', *Rural History* 4,2 (1993), 123-36; and Russell Davies, '*Secret Sins': Sex, Violence and Society in Carmarthenshire, 1870-1920* (Cardiff, University of Wales Press, 1996): 'secret sins' is a quotation from Evans. More recently, Philip Henry Jones, 'Scotland and the Welsh-language book trade during the second half of the nineteenth century', in *The Human Face of the Book Trade* (Winchester, St Paul's Bibliographies, 1999), 117-36, maintains that the classic 'Be This Her Memorial' understates the wiles and stratagems of the book canvasser in rural Wales – Evans's 'Seller of Bibles'.

Capel Sion

I

REDEMPTION

THERE WAS A young man whose piety was an adage, for his heart was filled with the glory of Sion. His manner was humble; on the Sabbath his face was habited in a religious smile and his lips framed the words "Big Man" or "White Jesus bach". Once in the Seiet the Ruler of the Pulpit said to him: "Eevan Rhos, man, mouth your experience." He answered: "Not saintly enough is my voice to be raised." Of him this was spoken: "He breathes to the Big Man."

A woman came to labour in his house and on his land. Her name was Hannah Harelip, and she was from the House of the Poor in Castellybryn. She was aspiring and covetous, and because Evan would not let her be mistress over all that was his, she oppressed him with the burden of her sin. But the Big Man freed Evan and joined him and Jane Pant in marriage.

On a day Evan viewed his possessions and was grieved that his wealth was so small. He said to himself: "Save much would I if I had a reaper and binder, and, dear me, there's a mouthful of butter I churn. Glad would I be of a machine separator." At nightfall he came into the house and commanded his servant Hannah Harelip to put axle grease on his Sabbath boots and on his leggings, and he went to the edge of the pond and cleaned his face. Early on the morrow – which was the Saturday of Barley – he rode forth on his pony to Cardigan, and before he entered the town he prayed in these words: "Big Man bach, don't you let any old woman cheat me now. Be with your Preacher in Sion. Amen." He stabled his pony and walked hither and thither in search of a wife.

At dusk he returned and said to Hannah: "A mishtress is coming to Rhos. What think you?"

"Misthir! Misthir!" cried Hannah. "Jokeful you are, now, indeed."

"Truthful is my saying," Evan answered. "Is she not Jane Pant? Nice little farm is Pant."

Soon it was noised abroad that Jane Pant was wedding Evan.

"Rich is Jane's father," said one.

Another remarked: "And husband ripe. Too religious is poor Evan to know what to do."

Now Hannah Harelip was a jealous woman, and she had set her affection to Evan; and her distress was sore that the man was going to marry a wife. She considered how to ensnare him, and it was so that she caused him to say to her: "Come you, small wench, and I will fondle you."

Hannah, who knew a little of the ways of man, ran from Evan as one alarmed, and as she moved her petticoats fell upon the ground, and she pretended to be greatly ashamed. "O mishtir bach," she cried, "here's dishonour. Bare as a bald pate am I." While she bent to settle her garments, Evan seized her, and whispered: "Wench very all right you are."

"Eevan Rhos," said Hannah, "frisky you feel, man."

After many days were passed, Hannah spoke to her master: "Well, well – mishtress of Rhos I shall be, for sure."

Her saying did not please Evan because she was become odious in his eyes. "What jobishness you speech, you bad boar! Go about your business in a great haste, you adder."

But Hannah neither departed nor remained silent: "Have I not served you as a woman?"

"Iss, indeed, laboured very well you have on my land. Don't you blobber old things, good maid. Off you, then."

"Lively are things in me, Mishtir bach. Better now that I sit in your pew in Sion."

"Go away, female," Evan rebuked Hannah. "An hireling you are. Born you were in sin. Has not the Big Man put a heated poker on your lips? Dirty smell of a mule, pray forgiveness for your awful act. High Father, an innocent boy bach was the male of Rhos until I was provoked by Satan's daughter."

Hannah would not give over pressing Evan to marry her. She said to him: "See you how I am swelling?"

"What's the matter with you? Disease of the swine?"

"No, no, man. Know you who made me so and such."

"Hannah Harelip," said Evan, "angry is the Big Man with you. I cannot say less."

"A lump you are for pleading" replied Hannah.

Evan's mind was afflicted. He admonished his servant in prayer and in her presence. "The strumpet from the House of the Poor accuses me in my face. Four large white shillings a week will she make me pay her. There's a wench for you, Big Man. But don't you now smite her dead with a stroke. Very forgiving man am I." To Hannah he said: "Evil female, I was not bad with you."

"Mishtir, no sense you cry," said Hannah.

"Close your head," Evan shouted. "You are less than a sour apple."

Hannah would not suffer the man's denial, and she piled up her courage, and stood up before Evan: "Mishtress of Rhos I shall be. Or large is the money I shall get. In the sessions I'll put you."

In that manner were Evan's blessings disturbed. Although Hannah was told that it is against God's will for a servant to charge her master, that God does not permit them who sit in the loft of Sion to murmur against them who sit on the floor and in the high places, she refused to be pacified or to give over her design.

There came an hour at which Evan governed his anger, and spoke kindly to Hannah. He said: "Tidy bit of hay in the narrow field."

"Iss. Thickish, indeed."

"Gather her in we will on the third day. Want you I do to go on top of the rick, and govern her will I on the ground."

"Very well, Mishtir," Hannah uttered.

Then Evan softened his voice: "How you was?"

"Pains are within," replied Hannah.

"Thought of this thing have I," Evan answered. "How speak you of a little wedding?"

"Mishtir bach, there's joy you spout. Well, well, now I shall be Hannah Eevan Rhos."

Evan proceeded: "Marry we will in the office of the old Registrar in Castellybryn as soon as the corn harvest is over. But listen you, now, wench: if persons inquire of you by whom you are big, say you by a boy of a weaver from Drefach. A religious sampler am I in Sion. Do you act then as I say."

At the gathering in of the hay, one said to Hannah: "Whose buttermilk have you been drinking?"

Another asked "The Schoolin's, or have you eaten brown sugar at Shop Rhys? Boys very maleish are the boys."

Hannah laughed without shame, and she answered as Evan had instructed her to answer.

As the last of the hay was pitched, Evan placed a ladder in the cart and rested it against the rick. "Come down, now, Hannah Harelip," he said.

The moment the woman's feet rested on the second rung, the horse that was in the cart stepped forward briskly, whereat Hannah fell upon the ground. Evan turned his face to the women who, scattered about the door of Rhos, were eating flummery oatmeal and skimmed milk, and cried loudly: "The wise women among you, come here. My servant Hannah has dropped the child of the weaver boy."

The women came, and having asked questions of Hannah and examined her, said: "Thanks to Big Man, the child is all right."

"Good that is," said Evan. "Sinful to destroy a life. Burning in hell is Pharaoh for his designs upon Moses bach."

The hay workers departed, and Evan and Hannah went into the house and at the end of their labour Evan raised his voice: "Not fit that you overwork on the morrow. Sit you down and rest." When the morning was come, and he had been into the fields, he said: "Bad jasto, great is the havoc the crows are making of my wheat."

"Useless is the scarecrow, then," said Hannah.

"Iss-iss, for sure. Large is the waste already. Shoot them I must. Dear me, now, clean you my little gun. Making a jaunt am I to ask Old Ianto of the Road to come and dig open the well."

Hannah did as she was bidden, and inasmuch as she was not familiar with guns she pressed her hand upon the trigger of it, and the gun fired. She trembled in her fear, and then she shrieked out that she was killed.

At midday, Evan came back and he said to her: "Sad is this. Go will I and bring the women."

Hannah stayed him: "No-no, Eevan bach. Healthy is my inside."

"Two, hap three crows," Evan wailed, "the powder and shots might slay."

Old Ianto of the Road opened the well – which is midway between the gate of the close and the door of Rhos – and there was much water in it; and the first day after the day it was opened a sheep fell therein. Evan lamented: "Big Man bach, why for you hold from me all that is profitable? Am I not of great regard in Sion?" He covered the mouth of the well with prickly shrubs and the shrubs also he covered with loose earth and stones, and it was so that the mouth of the well was like the ground about. Then he drew two wire fences from the edge of the flagstone – which is outside the door – to the farther brim of the well, and the width between the fences was the width of the well. Having done all that, he stood at the end of the fence, and beckoned his first finger to Hannah, and cried: "Come you here now, wench fach."

II
THE WORD

ACCORDING TO THE Word of Davydd Bern-Davydd, the Respected of Capel Sion, which is in the parish of Troedfawr, in the Shire of Cardigan:

My text, congregation fach, is in Luke, the seventh chapter and the second after the tenth verse: "Now when He came nigh to the gate of the city, behold, there was a dead man carried out, the only son of his mother, and she was a widow: and much people of the city was with her." The second after the tenth verse in the seventh chapter of Luke, people: "Now when He came nigh to the gate of the city, behold, there was a dead man carried out, the only son of his mother, and she was a widow; and much people of the city was with her."

Search deeply into the verse will I. Going about preaching was the White Jesus bach. A student He was at this time, collecting for His College, like the students that come here from College Carmarthen and College Bala. Grand was the sermon He had worded at Capernaum. There's big the collection was. Then He said: "For sure me, go I will to Capel Moriah in Nain."

Was not Nain, people bach, a big town? Things very pretty were in the town. There were Capels in every part, and the largest was Capel Moriah Dissenters. Moriah had two lofts, and in front of the lower loft there was a clock cuckoo; and nice the ornaments in the ceiling were now. And there's a splendid pulpit, higher than even the roof of the heathen old Church. Boys bach, never have you seen such a Book of Words. The cover was of leather; not hard leather, but soft like Mishtress Bern-Davydd's Sabbath shoes. And he had clasps of brass, and at the beginning of him was written the names of all the Rulers of Moriah.

Between the Capel and the road, as we have in Sion, was the burial ground, which from end to end measured more than from Shop Rhys to the tree on which Dennis sinned. The place was so big that you could not see the other side. Larger than ten hayfields. And as full of graves as Ianto's field is of thistles. Very careful you had to be not to walk on the graves. Fuller, indeed, five over twenty times than the burial ground of Capel Horeb in Morfa.

Natty were the stones over the graves. Come with me, little men, and peep at them we will. Here is one above a Ruler of the Pulpit. Photographs of angels at the end of the stone. And what a big angel bach on the head. What is he doing? Sounding he is, indeed to goodness, the Harp of Gold. What is the name of the hymn the angel bach is toning?

> Guide me, O Thou great Redeemer,
>   Pilgrim through this barren land;
> I am weak, but Thou art mighty,
>   Hold me with Thy powerful hand;
>   Bread of Heaven,
> Feed me now and evermore.

What is the Ruler's name, say you? A surprise. Read you on the stone again. "Here sleeps Solomon, who reigned over Israel for twice twenty years."

Dear me, here is a nice stone and costly. This is over the perished body surely of a nobleman. Who was he? Hap he had a shop draper or a walk milk. Great he was in the Big Seat. "He died in the Big Man's arms," is the writing. O persons, shall that much be said of you? When you hear the trumpet noising over your grave, will you say: "I am ready, White Jesus bach?" Shall that be said of you, Dai Lanlas, after the report that Eynon Daviss made about you? A dirty black you was, man, to jeer at Capel Sion.

Come, let us leave fulbert Lanlas and read the stones and heed the flowers glass on the mounds. There is the Mishtress Simeon: "Be this her Memorial." Here is the grave of the religious little widow who gave her mite. "Let this be counted unto her for righteousness." A grand sampler was the widow. She gave her mite. Nanss Penfordd, one yellow sovereign and half a crown you gave last year to Sion, though you get a large pension. Isaac Brongest, man, increase your sacrifice, or complain to the Big Preacher I must.

What is this? An open grave. What are the names on the stone at the side? "Abram Shop Grocer, Nain." Was Abram religious? Great was the wealth he left his widow Esther. Ask askings we shall of the old gravedigger. There he is – a tallish man and hairless and his trousers are loosened because of the heat of the sun. Occupation very good is making graves. Digging the houses which shelter us between here and the Palace. Very happy are affairs in the grave, people.

"Fair day, little man, how you was then?"

"Good am I, strangers; and fair day to you. Where shall I say you hail from?"

"Boys bach from Capel Sion," we say. "Proud is the graveyard."

The gravedigger rests his chin on the end of the rod of his pickaxe and wipes the tobacco spittle from his chin. "Iss, man, when this coffin is covered, there will be no more room. Has not the Capel taken the spacious field of Eben son of Joseph? Elegant will be the to-do at the first opening."

"The hole is not very large," we say. "Be he for a maid now?"

"No-no, male. Though he is narrow, he is not for a maid."

"As you speak. Mouth who is perished."

"A young youth," the old gravedigger says. "The son of Esther the widow of Abram Shop Grocer."

"Don't say. When is the funeral, male bach?"

"This day, boys Capel Sion. An hour after dinner."

The gravedigger takes out his old watch. "One o'clock. Saint Shames will be praying in the house now. Tearful are Shames's prayers. And Luke will speak also."

"Who is Shames and Luke?"

Astonished is the gravedigger. "Dullish you are. Is not Shames the Ruler of Capel Moriah in Jerusalem? And Luke bach the Ruler of Capel Antioch? Tuneful and short and sweet preacher is Luke bach the Singer. Do you tarry here to listen to his sermon over the coffin in the Capel. Treat you will have."

He goes down into the hole and makes the walls straight. Listen, blockheads. Is he not singing one of Hawen's hymns? Hymner very religious is Hawen. Now he comes up and examines his watch. "Late is the funeral," he says. He stands on the hedge, but he sees no men and women walking and letting tears in their Sabbath clothes. He cries to Daniel bach Lions who is the Keeper of the House of the Capel: "Slow is the carcase in coming, Daniel, now." Daniel answers: "Iss, indeed, sent Abed have I to seek reasons."

The afternoon grows and no funeral. The day dims. We will stay on, companions, for are we not to hear Luke bach the Singer saying a sermon? Iss, then, we will stop.

So we tarry and ask more questions of the gravedigger. "Was this a promising young youth – the son of Esther the Widow of Abram Shop Grocer?"

"Indeed, iss. Home he was from College Jerusalem. Did he not drive out the Bad Man from the body of a servant woman who had spoken ill of a teacher in the College? Learned he was in the School of Sunday. What is the matter for the funeral not to come? Dear me, don't say that Esther the Widow of Abram has perished and will be put in the grave with her son! Maybe Shames has the spirit on him. Shames prays sometimes for a week without a stop."

Go we will to meet the funeral. But here is Abed bach coming on the Tramping road. His belly shivers like the belly of Rhys Shop when he was found sinning with Anna in the storehouse, and his thick lips are gaped like the lips of the Schoolin when he desires Ellen Felin.

"Boys, boys," he cries. "Are you waiting to see the funeral?"

"Iss-iss, man," we answer.

"Then there is no funeral to be," he says. "The son of Esther is not dead."

"Well-well?" we ask.

"He is risen."

"Don't murmur idly," says the gravedigger.

"Truth sure this is," replies Abed. "Esau and Jacob and Matthew and Job were carrying the coffin from the house into the hearse when the Big Jesus passed. He said to Esther: 'Why for you weep?' And Esther told Him how Abram was in the Palace of White Shirts and now that her son was gone also there was none to care after the Shop Grocer. The White Jesus bach called up to him Samuel Carpenter and commanded him to unscrew the coffin. The young youth was alive."

"Goodness all," says the old boy of a gravedigger. "Will He stay long in the land?"

O males Capel Sion, much was the noise in Nain that day. Samuel took away the coffin and the screws. Shames did not pray. Luke bach the short and sweet Singer put his funeral sermon in the backhead pocket of his preacher's coat.

While the young youth was preparing to go into the Shop, Esther his mother said to him: "Boy bach, do you remember perishing?"

He answered: "No."

"Do you remember Sam Carpenter measuring you for a coffin?"

"No."

"Do you remember the White Shirt?"

"No."

"Did you hear Jesus speaking to you?"

"Iss, iss. I heard Him in Eternity."

Glad was Esther the widow woman. "Don't you hasten away, people," she said. "Stay you, and I will brew tea and make pancakes."

And do you know, O creatures, no night followed that day in Nain. Men and women went about and abroad, saying one to another of this miracle which had taken place in the house of Esther Shop Grocer. For the Big Man had raised His voice to the Chief Angel: "Put another wick in the sun."

III
THE TREE OF KNOWLEDGE

WATKIN PENSARN DIED, and his children were: Ben, Dennis, Mari. Ben inherited Pensarn and also the Field of the Tree – which is on the edge of the moor – and the mud-walled cottage therein. Mari did not receive anything, because of her whorish ways: she had had seven children by seven men. But Ben showed kindness unto her: he made her a servant on his land and he let her abide in the cottage which is in the Field of the Tree.

Dennis dwelt in Glasgoed, which is in the valley. He did not inherit anything. In the safety of his thirty-eight acres of land, a living house and outhouses, and one hundred and ten sovereigns, he offended against Sion. So the Big Man was angered and caused him to be persecuted and to commit the sin whose awfulness is above all other sins. The period of his infliction began when he rented the Field of the Tree from Ben and repaired the hedge around it and strewed manure on the floor of it, saying: "A hayfield will I make of the place bach." Before long he beheld that a narrow path was trodden down between the gate and Mari's house. His mind became stormy, and he shouted: "Mari, now, indeed, where you was? Why for you mess my hay?"

Mari moved to him.

"Blasted you are, bad wench, in my small eyes," Dennis cried. "Full of frogs is your carrion."

"This one moment, Dennis bach, windy you are" Mari replied. "Say you why to me."

"What you walk upon my grass? See you that you spoil my hay! A nasty lizard, dear me, you was."

"Vexed is your head," Mari answered. "Do you, Dennis Glasgoed,

33

show me how to reach the road."

Having abused his sister with these words: "Speech like an old crow you do," Dennis lifted the gate and the gate posts from the gap which was in the hedge and thereon he raised a wall of earth and stones, and into this new wall he cunningly contrived broken glass. Mari climbed over the hedge at another place and soon she made a deep opening in it. One night a cow came into the field and feasted. Dennis wept when he viewed the havoc the animal had made and spoke harshly to Mari; and as he spoke his rage was increased that there was another path between the house and the spring which yields fresh water.

"Sober serious," said Mari, "what does the man bach want? Weary am I of life. Do I not wish I was a hundred years ago?"

"Walk you away from here," Dennis answered. "Destroyer very terrible you are."

Dennis measured the length and breadth of the pathways and he thought out the bulk of hay he had lost, and the bulk was as much as two persons can pitch twice from field into cart. That knowledge pained him, and he went up to Ben: "Jasto, now, cheated me you have over the old field."

"Boy bach Glasgoed," said Ben. "Mouth you like that, for sure. Open wider the back of your head."

"The house in the field you give to Mari. There's a serpent is the shipsy."

"Is not the Big Man's curse on Mari, Dennis? Does He not torment her breast with an ulcer?"

"No care have I for that," cried Dennis. "Messed my hay bach she has. Nice grass there was in the paths."

"Well, you don't mean."

"Look you, iss-iss. But loutish you are. Shake yourself in my favour."

"Come you into the parlour bach," said Ben, "and I will hold forth." Therein Ben spat upon the floor and knelt. This is what he told God: "A black of a donkey was Cain. Brothers we all are, little Big Man. Dennis Glasgoed is here. Solemn is the thing that has happened to his hay. Be with your son in Sion. Amen." Before he arose he opened his eyes and he placed a finger and a thumb above his hairy nostrils and blew the residue therefrom upon the floor. Presently he charged the cast of his face with grief; and he spoke:

"Certain, Dennis Glasgoed. Cheapish is the little field."

Dennis understood: "A cunning herring you are."

"Speak you do like that. Well-well."

"Well-well?"

"Pay you me one sovereign and a half a sovereign every year and Mari's house you shall have," said Ben.

"Big Father, no-no! Poor am I."

"Losing very great am I to give you the house. But are you not my brother?"

"Half a yellow sovereign, Ben bach nice. Not worth killing is the hay. Cart a load of coals I will, too."

"No, man. Farewell, now."

Dennis rented Mari's house for fifteen shillings and a load of fairly turned dung, wherefore he devised a lying scheme; he said to Mari: "Stir off. Savage is the bull that I put in your house."

"Stir will I," replied Mari, "the minute I hear the noise of his coming."

When Dennis was returned to Glasgoed his wife Madlen was perturbed and in much fear. "Horrible is this. Guiltless am I."

"What is the matter with the strollop? Be you hasty," said Dennis.

"Perished is the ass fach."

Dennis did not chasten his wife. "Where is the carcase?"

"Sure me," Madlen answered, "boiling is the head for the pigs."

"Fool of a squirrel! Do you that, for why? Talk where the ass is."

"In the milk house is the body bach, covered with my petticoat."

Dennis put the ass in a sack which had held white flour and which was whitened therewith, and the next night he took the ass and also a pickaxe and a shovel to the Field of the Tree. He dug a hole in the ground and when he reached the water which flows into the spring, he hung the sack on the Tree and put the ass in the hole. As he was coming away, he said to himself: "Turks are persons, and robbers. Ben will take from me all that I have. Mari pilfers two pitches of my hay."

He walked down straightway into the Tramping road, and on all sides and around him he heard noises; he lifted his eyes and saw birds passing between him and the moon. He crawled over the last hedge into the road, and his gaze fell upon a shadow moving on the face of it. He was terrified, and he cried: "Jesus nice, boy bach going to Capel is here. Grand is your son in Sion. Amen." Dennis hasted onward and he remembered that he had left his sack on the Tree, and when he came back with the sack, the shadow was no longer on the road. Then he weighed that which he had seen and heard, and he imagined that the flying creatures were his enemies in the dress of birds, that the shadow was the Ruler of Sion; that the birds and the Ruler were scheming to take from him all that he had. In the darkness of Glasgoed he lit a tallow candle and counted his sovereigns and separated them evenly into four lots. He discovered Madlen's legs and removed therefrom the woman's stockings, and he also drew off his own stockings, and in each stocking he placed his money as he had divided it. Before he set out to bury his gold in four different parts, he cut his beard close to his skin, so that none of his enemies should know him. At dawn he brought forth his money and hid it in fresh quarters; and throughout that day he numbered and renumbered his cattle and his pigs and his hens, and he thought out the value of his crops. That night he would not go up to his bed. He cried to Madlen: "Where you was?"

"Hearing you am I, Dennis bach the husband," Madlen said. "Rest you, indeed."

"Listen to my tongue."

"Speak, then, boy bach."

"Have the nice pigs eaten their fill?"

"Iss-iss."

"Hungry are their sad grunts. Take food to them, you concubine."

Madlen put barley meal into a bucketful of skimmed milk and gave the pigs to eat.

"Wasteful you are, old female," said Dennis. "Bulging with potatoes is your stomach."

"Only three, man bach, and a little buttermilk. Empty was my belly."

"Not a yellow sovereign shall I have," Dennis moaned. "A wanton bitch you are."

"Dennis bach, don't say!"

"Speak I so, iss-iss. Thin are the creatures, and you eat rare potatoes and buttermilk."

Dennis opened the door of the lower end of his house and disturbed his hens which were roosting on the rafters. "Is not the cheatful Rachel Hens coming tomorrow?"

"Don't you let your small guts worry you," said Madlen. "Fat enough are the hens."

"Clap your mouth. Thin are the hens. Starving. Are not their bones like the blade of a scythe?"

Madlen stepped up to her bed. Dennis stayed at the door, and peered through the latch-hole. He wailed in this fashion: "Two pitches of hay do I lose because of the dirty Mari."

"Stiff is the head of the madam," Madlen said. "Herd her away with a rod. Put a pitchfork into her eyes."

"Hist!" Dennis cried. "They are after my yellow sovereigns!" He stood on the threshold and spoke: "Well, boys bach, what for you are here? Red money have I. No white silver. Religious boys bach you are. Iss-iss. Fair night, persons Capel Sion. Take you Madlen if her you desire. Do with her in the cowhouse. Madlen, go now with the boys. No yellow sovereigns, indeed to goodness, have I. Did not my ass perish? ... Madlen, a bitch you are. Tell them you did of the holes of my gold."

"Safe is your large gold, Dennis bach," Madlen replied.

"Told the boys you did. Robbed me you have."

"Where have I robbed you?"

"Iss-iss. Spout the places of my yellow money? In the potato field?"

"No, Dennis, now –"

"In the rick? Bad if my rick fires this night."

"Look you, sleep."

"Where have you hidden my gold? Half one hundred sovereigns you have pilfered from me. All my sovereigns bach are gone. And their number was above the number of stones in the burial ground."

Madlen shuddered: "Wait small minutes."

Dennis seized Madlen's body and he held it as one holds a battering ram and he beat the head against the wall, saying: "Yellow sovereigns you have thieved. And red pennies. And white silver. My creatures' food is in your belly. An old thief you are. Two pitches of hay Mari spoiled. Two big pitches of my hay bach. Sorrowful is this. All are in array against me."

He took a sheet from the bed and walked to the Field of the Tree, and he threw dry earth at Mari's window.

Mari answered: "Boy bach come to court?"

Dennis moved to a place where Mari could not see him, for the moon was full, and he falsified his voice: "Iss, now. Then, wench nice, come to the door."

Mari arrived at the door and this is what she saw: a figure covered in a white sheet. She howled loudly and her mind became disordered.

In the evening of the day the young men and the young women coming home from the Seiet saw a shadow on the face of the Tramping road, and howsoever hard they searched no one could find a cause for it. They were disquieted. One cried at the top of his voice: "A sign from the White Jesus bach!" and he sent three others to gather the most religious men in Sion to witness this thing. The religious men came and took counsel of one another, and the Respected Bern-Davydd said: "Blockheads you are, for sure. Find out we will what makes the old shadow."

So the people walked hither and thither and in the fulness of time they came to the Field of the Tree, and from the tree hanged the body of Dennis Glasgoed. It was covered in a sheet and the wind swayed from side to side.

"Dennis, indeed, what for you do this?" said Ben Pensarn. "The Fiery Pool is the cost of your sin."

Davydd Bern-Davydd spoke: "Like hogs do the wicked perish. Don't you touch the crow, Ben Pensarn. Your flesh is too saintly."

Dennis hanged on the tree till the evening of the next day; as soon as the sun was down Ben called up to him two men, and he gave them a saw which had two handles, and he commanded them: "Go you up and kill branch of the tree from which my sinful brother Dennis is hanging. Take you the rope fach from his neck and bring him whole to me. And carry a lantern with you, because tight is the knot that chokes a man. Be you careful you do not walk overmuch on the hay."

The men felled the tree and took away the rope from Dennis's neck, and they carried the body on a wheelbarrow to Glasgoed and rested it on the floor by the body of Madlen.

At the return of day Ben Pensarn harnessed a horse into a cart, in the head of which he put Dennis's hens and in the back of which he put Dennis's pigs, and he drove to Castellybryn and sold the hens and the pigs. Thereafter he took possession of all that was Dennis's – except the gold which remains hidden – saying: "My brother's keeper am I."

IV
THREE MEN FROM HOREB

WHILE ENOCH THE Teller of Things was shearing the ends of his beard for the Sabbath, word came to him that his son Ella, who dwelt in Morfa, was dead. On the morrow he bowed his head in Sion until the time came for him to say the orderings of the service, and when he had said all that was to be said, he expressed his grief: "Flown over Jordan in a White Shirt is Ella bach. Bad was his illness. Nasty is old decline. Come you all to his large funeral at Capel Horeb –"

The Respected Bern-Davydd put out his right arm. "Indeed now, Enoch," he said, "wait a bit, man. Why for you say Horeb? In Capel Sion must Ella be buried. Horeb, ach y fi."

"Iss; gate-post is your head, Enoch," cried Amos Penparc. "Have you no pride in the Glory of Sion? More graves there are in Sion than turnips in two rows."

"Go you, then," commanded Bern-Davydd, "and bring the perished corpse to Sion. Bring him before he stinks. In this way says the Big Man, little animals: 'Give to the Capel what belongs to the Capel, and there shall be laughing in the Palace, Bern bach.'"

Old Enoch borrowed a hay wagon, the inside of which he furnished with two patchwork quilts and a pillow, and the outside of which with black cloths and strips of black crêpe. To Mati, Ella's wife, he said: "You hog, give you me the corpse of my son bach."

Mati answered him: "Lived have I here all my days. My children were born here and they converse with the Big Man in Horeb. In Horeb Ella shall be put into the pit."

Enoch did not heed the words of Mati his daughter-in-law: he went into the parlour and took the body of Ella and put it in his wagon and he covered it with a patchwork quilt; and on the flat road, which brings you back to Sion, he sat on the shaft, his short bandy legs dangling loosely. He wept in the face of passers-by until his eyes were sore: "Man that is perished is in the cart, people bach. He is my son Ella. Wet will be the tears at his funeral. There's a prayer he was! And a big friend of the Little Jesus bach." He also sang: "In the big floods and swells there is none to hold my head, but my beloved husband Jesus, who died upon the Wood."

He brightened the boots which were on Ella's feet and he shaved Ella's face; and he laid the body on a table and put an open Bible on its belly; and at the side of it he placed an empty coffin, the lid of which was ornamented with gold handles and the plate of which was engraved with Ella's name and age – which was forty-seven years – and a good account.

On the Wailing Night old Enoch stayed by his son, howbeit one asked him to sup of buttermilk or tea or to eat of white bread and butter or bread and cheese. As the praying men and singing men and women were mourning Ella in prayers and hymns, Shon Daviss – a high man in Capel Horeb – opened the door and on the threshold he cried solemnly: "Here's horror. Big Man is looking down and weeping. Male of Horeb was Ella. Awful is the cost you will have to pay for this sin."

"Speech you do like a billhook," said Bern-Davydd.

"No, man," replied Shon Daviss; "serious for sure. Come have I to talk that the boy bach be buried in Horeb."

The words angered the congregation. They said: "Scarce are the graves in the new burying land. Respected Bern-Davydd, speak spiteful phrases to the old cat fach."

Bern-Davydd turned his face upon Shon Daviss, rebuking him: "Boy of the Bad Man, be you in a hurry to go in a haste. Jasto now, give him a kick somebody in the backhead."

"Robber of Sion, away, indeed" some of the congregation shouted. "Or much damage we shall do to you."

The man from Horeb ran away from the house; and the next day Old Enoch prepared Ella for burial: he stripped him of his clothes and put on him a White Shirt of the Dead. The material of the garment was flannel made by Ellen Weaver's Widow, and it was marred by neither spot nor blemish. The flannel at the wrists of the garment had been decorated by an embroiderer, and the hem of the skirt had upon it fluffed sheep's wool. Having ended, old Enoch lifted his hairy cheek to God, and opened his lips: "Big Man bach, religious am I. Shall I button the White Shirt?" He waited and God spoke to him privately. "All right, as you speak, Big Man; quickly Ella will become naked when he hears the trumpet. Quicker than anyone in Sion."

A sinful thing happened: while Ella's coffin rested on ropes at the edge of the grave three men from Horeb arrived without the gates of Sion, and the leading man, who was Shon Daviss Shop Boots, shouted: "Ho-ho, sinners Capel Sion, Ella must sleep in Horeb. Come we have for the perished corpse."

In their confusion the people – men and women and small children – who were come to weep and mourn, fell apart into a lane, wherewith the three men passed thereupon to the place where the coffin was.

Bern-Davydd's rage kindled. He screamed: "The son of Enoch shall come up from Sion! Foxes of strumpets you are, boys Horeb."

"Ho-ho!" cried Shon Daviss. "Askings we have put to our Respected, and great is his understanding. Divide you, people, and the coffin bach we will take with us."

"Hares of Horeb," said Bern-Davydd, "take off your hands. Stoutish shall the Glory of Sion grow."

"Stealing from Horeb you are a perished corpse," answered Shon Daviss. "We shall take him away. Come, boys bach, let us put him in the cart. Religious was Ella; shall he be buried among calves?"

"Away, turks of mackerel," Old Enoch cried. "Borrowed a gambo I did to bring Ella to Capel Sion."

The three men from Horeb lifted the coffin; and as they were doing so, Enoch struck Shon Daviss with the gravedigger's pickaxe. The coffin dropped upon the ground and the lid of it came asunder. Shon's temper heightened. "Fiery Pool!" he cursed. "Knock you will I this one small minute."

Old Enoch shivered because of the blow delivered upon his forehead by Shon Daviss; and he fell into the grave.

There was much disorder, during which the three men from Horeb raised the body of Ella out of its coffin and ran away with it and put it on the straw that was on the floor of the cart; and one of them said to the mare between the shafts: "Gee-gee, go on."

The people of Sion, awakened to the value of this that was done against their burial ground, chased the men from Horeb, and as they could not overtake them, they climbed over hedges and went across the fields. In that manner the men of Sion came upon the men of Horeb and stopped them; and the battle went hard against Horeb.

The body of Ella was brought back to Sion in the dim light, and the gravedigger, after Bern-Davydd had prayed that the Big Man would regard mercifully the blemishes on Ella's White Shirt, put a ladder down into the grave, saying: "Come you up, now, Enoch bach."

V

THE PILLARS OF SION

SILAH PENLON WAS a doltish virgin. People who were bound to Capel Sion said to her mother:

"Large is the Big Man's curse upon you, Becws Penlon."

"What for you speak wild, people bach?" answered Becws. "Wench fach very tidy is the wench fach."

The people rated her in a high voice. They said: "Not pious is your brawl. There's vile is the backhead of your mouth for you to talk like that."

"Can I say, 'Be you familiar indeed, then, Silah fach'?" Becws returned.

"What is the matter with the old woman? Tell me you!" cried the people. "Full of sin was your old belly when you bore the wench. Explain, dear me, to us, Becws fach, the name of your sin and say longish prayers for you we will."

Becws's spirit lowered: she was apprehensive that she would trespass unwittingly, and that the men who sat in the Big Seat in Capel Sion would inform against her to God. So she fashioned this prayer, which she spoke from time to time:

"Big Man bach, an old disorder you put on Silah. Do you lift him now from her. Wench fach very tidy is the wench fach also. Is she not a bulky age? Was she not born when the Respected Davydd Bern-Davydd came to Sion, thirty and five years ago? Stay with your son nice in the Capel and with all the boys bach of the Big Seat. Amen."

God withheld His ear from Becws, and He fixed a further affliction to her daughter: He made Silah's mind stubborn and the virgin behaved as one who is dumb; and she would not entreat the Man of

Terror to abate His anger against her. Becws was in fear and dread, and she bared her arm and stripped Silah and beat her; and the dirty spirits were strong within Silah, and though she wept she did not make any sound. Becws thought out another prayer, for her heart yearned for Silah: "Speech Him advice to Becws fach Penlon, Big God. Solemn serious, act I will as He orders. Be near to His Son in Sion, and remain with the religious men of the High Places. Amen."

In the night she dreamt that her goat had got dry without reason, and after she had punished her with the handle of a spade, a scarlet crow flew forth from out of the animal's mouth. Becws interpreted the dream thus: the goat was Silah, and the scarlet crow was the Bad Man from the Fiery Pool, and the handle of the spade was Bern-Davydd. Wherefore on the Sabbath she took out her funeral garments and put them on Silah, whom she brought into Sion; and mother and daughter sat among the hired people in the loft.

The rage of the congregation was high when they comprehended the meaning of this abomination.

"Ach y fi!" said one. "A sick old mouse is Becws."

"Out of her head is the female," said another. "Silah was conceived in brimstone. The dolt's hair is the colour of flames."

The praying men said: "Not right is this, people bach, dear me. Come, now, then, the most religious of us off will go and make phrases to the Respected."

They went into the House of the Capel, and the chief of them was Amos Penparc, whose riches were above any other man on the floor of Sion, and whose piety was established. Amos stood on the threshold, and the lesser praying men stayed on the flagstone, which is without the door.

"Hello, here!" said Amos. "Not wishful, religious Respected, are we to disturb his food eating, but there's grave are the words in my head."

Bern-Davydd answered. "Come you, boys bach Capel Sion, the son of the Jesus bach will always hearken to you."

"Well-well, then," said Amos Penparc. "What he does not know that Silah the mad bitch sat in Sion this day?"

"Indeed to goodness, Amos bach! Speak you like that, I shouldn't be surprised," replied Bern-Davydd.

"And did I not observe the female Becws praying her own prayer while he was mouthing to the Great One?" said Amos.

"Don't speak any more, Amos Penparc," said Bern-Davydd. "Retch my old food I will. Read you the Speech Book for a small time bach."

Bern-Davydd finished his eating, and he lifted his voice: "Don't say!"

"Iss, iss, Respected."

"Can a carrot turn colour?"

The praying men were amazed.

Amos Penparc said: "Is not Silah counted an offender in the Palace of White Shirts?"

"Smell is Silah in the Big Man's nose," said Bern-Davydd.

"Iss, little Respected," said Amos. "Fall upon us He will. He will smoulder our little ricks of hay. Speak him then what shall our cattle eat."

At the close of the day Bern-Davydd, in the presence of all the congregation, addressed the men of the Big Seat: "Now, then, boys Capel Sion, make proof about Silah the daughter of Becws. Amos Penparc, start, man bach."

"Well, now, indeed, no," said Amos. "Right that the Religious of the Pulpit says sayings."

"Much liking has the Big Man for you Amos," said Bern-Davydd.

Amos rose and turned his bland countenance and unclouded eyes upon the assembly, and fastening his coat over his beard, he spoke: "Important in my pride is Sion. In Sion the Big Man's son dwells." Then sang Amos Penparc: "Lord bach, lessen your fury and depart not from us. Has not the Respected made us very religious? Is not the Capel like a well-stocked farm? The seating places are as full as the stables of the Drovers' Arms on an old fair day. And there's rising will be from the burial ground when Gabriel bach blows his gold trumpet: there will come up more people than I have sheep on the moor. Good is the Big Male to his photographs." Amos ceased his song. "But, people bach, sinful was Becws to bring her mad harlot into Sion. Lots of talk nasty there will be. Can corn grow from the seed of wasteful old thistles? Are mad bitches a glory unto Sion? How says the Respected: 'Bad old smell in the Big Man's nose is Silah'? The Temple must be cleansed, indeed, now."

"Wholesome, male man of Penparc, are your words," said the Respected Bern-Davydd. "Close my eyes I will now and say affairs to the Big Man: Jesus bach, wise you are to be with Amos Penparc.

Full of wisdom is Amos, and his understanding is higher than the door of Sion, deeper than the whiskers under his waistcoat. Four pillars hold up the loft of Capel Sion, and not one is as strong as Amos. Lias Carpenter can hew the pillars with his saw, but who can hew through Amos? Speak now to us about cleaning the Temple. Mad is Silah, and did not Becws her mother bring her into Sion? Disgrace very bad is this. Lewd was the wench's behaviour, Jesus. Busy am I thinking out sermons, so you come down and tell orderings to Amos Penparc. Amen."

Bern-Davydd's praise of Amos Penparc was spread abroad, whereof Becws got ashamed of that which she had done.

"Why you are without sense, idiot?" she said to Silah.

Silah did not answer.

"The concubine fach!" said Becws. "A full barrow of sin is in your inside. Open your neck, you bull calf. Have you not made me wicked in the sight of Sion?"

Becws was angry that her daughter was speechless and she did not give her food for two days, and as Silah was yet stubborn she placed her in the pigsty and tied her hands together behind her back so that she could not open the door, and she said to her: "Stay here, you scarlet crow; eat from the trough and lie with the swine."

Silah licked from the trough, and lay with the pigs. The people had tidings of her punishment. Some came and hid in secret places about Penlon, and they came away and bore witness how that they had heard her babbling in this fashion to the pigs: "Pigs bach, fetch a little barrow and take away the sin from my inside. Is there a haywaggon large enough to hold the sins of Bern-Davydd?"

"Take you no record, dear hearts, of the jolt-headed wench," Becws pleaded with them. "Without sense she is."

The people noised Silah's blasphemy, and Becws removed her daughter from the pigsty, for she was afraid that the dirty spirits would go in and possess the swine.

"Come you into the house, you yellow pig," she said. "And clap your lips about the terrible Bern-Davydd. Is not Amos Penparc discussing you with Jesus?"

Silah did as she was commanded, and she was as dumb as she was before.

Amos addressed the congregation of the Seiet: "Well-well, with God have I been. The Big Man came to the side of my bed. 'Why for is your small face so down, Amos Penparc?' He said. 'Have I withheld your crops or have I displeased you?' 'Not for myself am I so low,' I answered. 'For sure, no, son bach. Has not the Respected reported well of you to me?' He said. 'Grand preacher is Bern-Davydd,' I talked. 'Say you quick in a hurry what is the matter with you. Don't rouse my temper,' He ordered. 'Sion is foul.' I sobbed, little people. And I told him how the mad bitch Silah had sat in the loft. Surprised was the Big Man. 'Boy bach, you don't mean!' He cried. 'Iss, indeed, old Silah Penlon made joy of her conception and I put my finger on the child in her belly.' 'Dear me!' I said. 'Iss, Amos bach; say you to the Capel that the evil wench must cleanse the saintly abode, even the roof of the Temple. But she must not go up into my son's pulpit.'"

The religious men answered Amen.

Silah came to free Sion of her filth, and Becws was with her; and in the middle of the day Amos Penparc entered to look into Silah's labour, and he was not pleased that Becws was there also.

"Why don't you obey, you strumpet born of a donkey?" he cried in his wrath. "Hard is your head. Cheating the Big Man of His price you are."

Thereafter Amos tended Silah in Sion, and watched that she did not go up into the pulpit.

The morrow of the tenth day after the day that Silah had begun to clean Sion, the congregation gathered in the burial ground to bury the body of a man, and as the people looked down upon the floor of the grave, behold, the earth was disturbed and there were foot-holes in the walls of it. The people were abashed and awed, because the dead man had lived without reproach. They drew to Amos Penparc, asking of him: "Amos the wise, make you explanations how this thing has come about." Amos exercised his mind. He replied: "A daughter of the Bad Man is in the Capel, and the last night old Satan came up from the Fiery Pool to converse with her."

"Sober, indeed," said one, "did the black Satan enter the Capel? How now?"

Amos admonished this person: "Like a squirrel of an infidel you are. Sion would consume Satan."

In the middle of the twelfth week Sion was whole again. That which the Big Man had said to Amos Penparc was come to pass. All of the congregation were very proud. The praying men blessed the

Lord, and the singing men and women sang His fame.

On a night Bern-Davydd assembled the men of the Big Seat, and to them he said: "Boys bach, religious we are in Sion. Fitting now will be to show respect to the Big Man. Amos Penparc, give advice to us."

"'Search the Scriptures,' say the Book of Words," Amos answered. "Grand will be to hold a Questioning the Problem gathering. Little ruler, he will be the questioner."

Sion took Amos's counsel and ordained this religious feast on the Day of Christmas, which was three months away; and the men cunning and subtle in the Word were bidden to the loft of Capel Sion to have their knowledge tested by Bern-Davydd.

As the day of the feast came near, Silah's size enlarged.

Becws was uneasy; she moaned on the Tramping road that her daughter was possessed of many satans. Moreover she heated an iron rod with fire and laid it on Silah's navel. But the satans did not go away; and Silah's size continued to increase.

Now in the dark Silah left her mother's house and journeyed through the fields to Penparc, and at the door of the stable she made a noise like the bray of a mule. Amos came out to her and opened the door of the stable, and he said to her: "Now, well-well, Silah Penlon, how was you, then?"

Silah put out her arms and drew Amos to her; and she uttered words: "Boy bach nice is Amos." Amos was dismayed and he could not free himself from her embrace. Before the darkness got thin he laid a snare for her: "Come you here before the twilight of the third day, Silah fach, and a large little reward will I give you. Go you out, now, through the little window."

Silah went abroad in the neighbourhood and she laughed in the face of the people and spoke foolishly in their hearing. She was joyous, though she did not know anything. Becws thanked the Lord loudly: was He not repenting of His works against Silah?

On the eve of the twilight of the third day Silah stood at the door of the stable of Penparc and she made a noise like the bray of a mule. Amos came out of his house and there was with him Bern-Davydd, and to him he said: "What's that old shouting, I don't know?" and they two walked up to Silah.

Bern-Davydd seeing her, said: "Go you off, you mad bitch of hell fire."

Silah did not attend to his words. She put out her arms. "Boy bach nice is Amos Penparc," she cried.

Amos was vexed. "What for you mean, you clobstick?" he said. "Religious, witness him that I am falsely accused."

"What you call?" said Bern-Davydd to her. "Away you off now, or for sure kick your teeth will I."

As Silah did not move Bern-Davydd threw her upon the ground. The woman rose, turned, and ran. Bern-Davydd and Amos followed her and pelted her with stones, and with clods of earth. At Penlon, Amos said to Becws: "Shout you up your swine Silah."

Silah came.

"Deny, you cow," said Amos to her, "that I have been bad with you. Jesus bach, if I have mixed my flesh with the flesh of any old female, make you a small sign."

He gazed around for a sign, and here was none; and he congratulated the Big Man that He was on the side of righteousness.

Then he counselled with Bern-Davydd, and they two caused a seat to be set for Silah in the cow-stall, and they placed over her neck a hempen halter, the ends of which were attached to an iron staple driven deep into the wood of the stall.

Silah bit through the rope and thieved the saw of Lias Carpenter, and she came by stealth into Capel Sion, and sawed through each of the four pillars; and no one saw her going in or coming out. In the morning the subtle men congregated in the loft. The pillars parted, and the loft fell, but Amos Penparc was without hurt.

VI
THE WIDOW'S MITE

CONCERNING THE COW Gwen of Esther Crooked Tygwyn –
Tygwyn is on the zig-zag lane that goes up from Penparc. It came to
be that the cow would neither eat nor give any milk, and she did not
chew her cud. For those reasons Esther was troubled in her mind.
She spoke to Morgan her husband: "What is the matter with the cow,
I don't know. Hap she wants the bull bach. Drive her now to the
black bull of Amos."

Morgan sat on a three-legged stool and his grey hands were spread
out over a peat fire. He groaned because of the cancer which was in
his throat.

"What for you are a botherer, the man?" said Esther. "Old evil is
in your flesh. Go off this one minute."

Morgan herded Gwen to the close of Penparc and he acquainted
Amos with the purpose of his errand. Upon that Amos brought
forth his bull, at the sight of which Gwen quailed, because for
bigness and strength the animal surpassed all others in the land
round about, and fled.

"Very odd, dear me, is your cow, Morgan," said Amos.

"Iss-iss," Morgan answered. "Sick is the cow fach. Does she not
hold back her milk?"

"Talk you like that, the awful black," said Amos. "Scampish you
are, bad boy, to bring your old cow to defile my black bull. Will I not
get much yellow money for him at the Fair Harvest? For shame
indeed, Morgan Tygwyn."

Whereupon Morgan humbled himself in the face of Amos; and he
went home and told Esther all of that Amos had spoken to him.

Hence the woman derided him that he had not devised deceits. "Speak you to him not about the largeness of the bucket that Gwen fills with milk? A blind sow is in your head."

Therefore Esther was perplexed and dejected, and she was distressed that the cow's life was in jeopardy. So she pondered; and while she pondered she put away the mess that was in the cowhouse and scattered clean straw upon the floor of the stall, and when she had spread a blanket over the straw, she brought Gwen therein, saying: "Lie you down, dear cow." Presently she gazed at the animal's udder, and beholding an ulcer upon it, she made a poultice from bread and water and with it she covered the wound. Having ceased her labours that day, she spoke these words to God: "Big Man, turn your think and don't destroy the cow Gwen. A fair woman am I in Sion, Jesus bach. Esther is my name, and is there not a little Esther in the Book of Words? Costly is Gwen. Three over fifteen sovereigns is the price of a cow like her, and no old luck money back. Little Big Farmer, make her healthy. Be with your boy bach in Capel Sion. Amen." Then she rested on a portion of the blanket and slept.

Two days and two nights was the period which Esther stayed by Gwen, and though she made a new prayer and covered the ulcer with many fresh poultices, the cow was not rid of her sickness. On that account Esther's ire livened up against Morgan, and she said to him that he had charged the cow with his disease. Morgan answered neither yes nor no, for his strength was as a little child's. After the heat of her passion was over, Esther meditated; in the morning she stirred early, and she clothed herself in her Sabbath garments and she journeyed to Castellybryn, to the house of Sam Warts, whose trade it is to buy cattle. Him she addressed: "Woe is in my stomach, man bach."

"Talk you about what?" said Sam.

"Don't he mock me, the good boy," Esther said. "Perishing is Morgan bach. Sober am I."

"Are we not all like little cattle? Iss, very well, woman fach, all of us shall wear the White Shirt fach."

"Wise is he, the male of the Big Man. Grand is his wisdom. Say him, God's servant, good sayings about Morgan."

"Stop you, now," said Sam; "the Meeting for Prayer is on the third night. Eloquent, for sure, shall my spoutings be for Morgan Tygwyn."

"Large thanks, Sam Warts," said Esther. "Comforted will Morgan be to see him before he crosses."

"Brisk am I, dear me, Esther Tygwyn."

"Serious, iss. Hap he likes to see Gwen. Cow fach very pretty is the cow fach."

"Talk you the age of the cow, Esther."

"Nine years, little son. But sell her I won't. Grand milcher she is."

"Pay I nice yellow sovereigns for her."

"The last day Morgan bach said: 'Going am I to the Palace, Esther. If you sell Gwen take her to Sam Warts, for the man is mighty in Capel Bethel, Castellybryn.'"

"And like that he said? His words I shall repeat to the One."

"Boy nice religious, iss-iss. Clap hands then, for five over ten sovereigns and the cow I shall bring him the first morning."

"Come will I and search over her," Sam answered.

"Clap hands, and half a yellow sovereign he shall have for luck."

"No, woman. The yellow money I have not in the pockets of my trousers."

That night Esther entreated the Lord: "Big Man All Right, mean is the scamp Sam. Close his eyes against the very small sore on Gwen's udder. Be with your boy bach in Capel Sion. Amen." In the day she opened the mouth of the cow and put grass between the lips and the teeth, and she also sprinkled white flour upon the udder.

Sam the cattle dealer came out of Castellybryn into the house of Esther, and he examined Gwen and rubbed away the flour that was on the udder; and his wrath against the woman was such that he dug a finger nail into one of the warts which was on his forehead, and he said to her that she had done more to provoke the Big Man's hate than even the sinners who mouth book prayers in the church.

His words caused Esther exceeding misery and she could not sleep, and at dawn she said to Morgan: "Shake your body you black of a turk." Morgan put clogs on his feet and a coat over his body, and when he had eaten of a little broth, Esther spoke to him: "Go you with the old cow beyond the moor and say to the people: 'Persons honest, boy bach am I from Capel Sion. The little cow is all that I possess, and see you how she is perishing. Bad cancer, too, is eating my neck. Give you me, then, a little halfpenny or a little penny.' Walk you off."

The man did put a cord over the horns of Gwen and he led her over the moor and into the road of Morfa; and to all the people he met he spoke the words which Esther had ordered him to speak; and as he passed forward men and women moved to the middle of the way and remarked his height – he was a very high man – and one said to another: "His coffin shall be long and shallow." He journeyed forth four days; and the sum of money which he gathered was over five shillings. So it was that the sickness of death gripped him; he could not speak and he walked as walks one who is diseased in both feet. In the middle of the fifth day he died. Then an awful rage possessed Esther, and she put a rope over the forelegs and a rope over the hind legs of her cow. The end of the rope that was over the forelegs she fixed to a wood peg which was driven into the floor of the field near to a tree of sour apples, and the end of the rope that was over the hind legs she fixed to a bough of the tree.

While Gwen was perishing Esther cast off all her clothes and sat upon the heap of newly broken stones which was against her house, and she answered passers to who inquired why she conducted herself so strangely: "Very nude am I after the flying of Morgan bach." Many, in their pity, gave her money.

In the morning she loosened the ropes which held Gwen to the tree and to the floor, and she stripped the animal of its hide; when she was finished and had made the hide into a bundle, she went outwards and into the houses of the district, and to some of the inhabitants she said: "Having gone is my cow fach. Give you me a little red penny"; to others she said: "In his White Shirt is Morgan Tygwyn, the male of mine. Give me a red halfpenny." She assumed grief, and in the sight of every one she laid bare the affliction which made her crooked. She travelled to the Hills of Boncath, the Shores of Morfa, and to Castellybryn. She stumbled back to Tygwyn on the twelfth day, and she was possessed of two sovereigns, above the sum which Morgan had gathered and the sum which she got for Gwen's hide.

Esther rested and slept. In the day, after supping of bread in tea, she set out to the house of Abel Shones, who is the giver of Poor Relief. She said to Abel: "My heart bach, get him a coffin for my male husband."

"What for you babble?" answered Abel. "Put your money in your apron and take him to Lias Carpenter."

"Oh, there's a boy bach nasty you was," said Esther; "poorer am I than a fish," and she wept in Abel's hearing.

Abel came up to Tygwyn to view and measure Morgan, and as he drew aside the sacks which covered the body, lo, worms crept in and out of the mouth and out of the eyes of the dead man.

VII
CALVARY

PEDR, THE EARTH of the altar which he named Calvary and on which he addressed God still on his garb, came down from the moor to warn the people of Sion that their sins were so heavy and many that the Big Man could neither weigh them nor create bags enough into which to put them. Of his words the congregation were careless.

Lloyd Schoolin cried to him: "What about a bit of a sermon, now, Pedr?"

"Not a preacher very grand am I," answered Pedr. "Do you not listen to the Respected Bern-Davydd?"

"Boy, boy," said Lloyd Schoolin, "preacher all right you are."

"Good your words, dear me," replied Pedr. "Glad would I be to spout in a religious capel."

"For sure, iss," said the people; and they feigned to be serious.

"Come you, now, to the Garden of Eden and speech preaches to us," said Lloyd Schoolin.

In the Garden of Eden Pedr stood on the trunk of a fallen tree. "Now, then," he said, "sing you a nice hymn."

Lloyd Schoolin splayed his feet and sounded his tuning fork upon his blackened teeth; and the people having sung, Pedr placed his hand upon his nostrils, which were flattened against his lips, and prayed silently.

"Go on, Pedr," said Lloyd Schoolin. "Say the preach, man. Iss, people, a fool of a preacher is Pedr. Away we will go."

"No-no," Pedr urged. "Stay you and hear Pedr bach. The rage of the Big Man is as furious as the rage of the ram that slayed Hetti's child by Job Stallion."

"Now, Pedr, go slow. Old wench very bad is Hetti. Did not the Big Man make her mad? Go slow."

Pedr looked upon the people with concern. "This is what the Big Man talked to me: 'Grasping is the Ruler of the Pulpit. Always asking he is, Pedr bach, for yellow money. There's a boy he is for his pocket. And because I abhor Sion I have sent Davydd to judge there.'"

"Look you, Pedr," said the Schoolin, "sin you mouth."

One stood up behind Pedr and lit a match and held the flame of it at the fork of Pedr's legs, whereat the congregation laughed, Lloyd saying: "Jasto, indeed me, there's comic. An old sore the dull man will get. Wenches, look at her burning."

Pedr put out the burn and proceeded: "Sin to do this against a male. But, well-well, among Sinners am I. Tell you who shall wear the White Shirts of the Palace? Like this the Big One: 'Wickedness is in the burial grounds of Capel Sion. How can White Shirts grow out of wickedness?' Into the Fiery Pool you will be thrown. Amos Penparc robbed his own blood and sinned against Silah Penlon. Job Stallion kills his wife. Dan son of Shan was bad with his old mam. The Big One will loosen the sea of Morfa and the sea shall run up the moor and sweep down upon you, and you will all be thrown into a Pool filled with brimstone and water, and the water will sting you more fiercely than the brimstone. Pedr bach will stand on Calvary, and my flesh shall be unsinged. The little white Jesus says: 'You, Pedr, will bury the utterly dead after the Rising. I am not –'"

The people laughed scornfully.

"A black of a pig you are," said Lloyd Schoolin. "Pelt you we will with mess."

Some of the congregation tossed dung upon Pedr's face, and some derided him with their tongues and mocked him with distorted faces. Pedr did not try to evade any of the blows nor one handful of the mess which was aimed at him. "The Man of Justice will punish you for this. Pray the mess bach you shall for your fields. Very good am I in the Big One's eyes, and I shall live for ever. Off I will now and pray for Sion on Calvary the whole of this night and the next day."

Then went Pedr up to Calvary, and at the rising of the sun he paused in his prayer to refresh himself with a little water, and as he neared his hut he saw Lloyd Schoolin and Bertha Daviss parting at the entrance thereof. The Schoolin hasted towards the Roman trench. Pedr cried: "Stop, Schoolin bach. A warm male you are for flesh."

"Indeed, Pedr," answered Lloyd, "talk anything you are. Bad female is Bertha. Praying for her was I."

Pedr stood in Lloyd's path. "The Schoolin," he said, "timid is your nature."

"Iss, to goodness. A timid one bach am I. Depart I will now to open the School."

"Go you do into Bertha because the concubine is no longer fruitful. Evil is that in the eyes of the large Father."

"Look you, Pedr. Brawl not like that. Tempt me into the hut did the bitch. Did she not say: 'Come you into the hut. Pedr is praying this night. Ask you now for mercy for me. And don't you speak too loud, boy nice'?"

Lloyd listened to Pedr's words, and then he said: "Very religious I feel. A male very grand you are. Journey you down to the School House and discuss the White Evangel we will."

On the third night after Pedr had been to the School House, Lloyd said to Bern-Davydd: "To the door of the Abode I will walk with him for a little converse. Who shall help me if not the son of Jesus bach?"

"This is hearing so and such," said Bern-Davydd. "Sadness is in my heart also Mishtress Bern-Davydd says: 'Not respectable unto Sion is his preacher's coat, Respected'."

"Dear, dear. Order Enoch the Teller of Things I will to shout for a nice collection."

"No, don't you do that, Schoolin. The Big Man will not suffer His son to want."

"How would he say, then, if I gave him a silver crown to buy one?" asked Lloyd.

"Keep you the silver crown in the pocket of your trousers," said Bern-Davydd. "Fair night for now."

"Two silver crowns can I give," said Lloyd. "Two large silver crowns."

"Not needful for old money am I," Bern-Davydd declared. "Make you me take two silver crowns and half a silver crown. Well-well, all in the name of the Rich Man."

"Very Respected Religious," said Lloyd Schoolin, "keep him by me now. He knows that this is the truth that spouts from my head. A yellow sovereign has the tinker Pedr thieved from me."

"Lloyd Schoolin, wealth you have lost. Speak you about this."

"Pity I had for Pedr, and I placed food before him in my house."

"Dear me, and woe is me. Satan is Pedr. Does he not cry that you and Bertha Daviss go into his old hut?"

"There's a rotten turnip," said Lloyd. "The Religious Respected knows that my flesh is clean."

"Go up we will and speak hard to the iob," replied Bern-Davydd. "To the Lord you give three silver crowns, and send you a portion of pig's meat to the Mishtress. Tell her I will to boil the meat bach in the broth."

Bern-Davydd and Lloyd Schoolin and a great company went up to the moor. Pedr was on Calvary and he saw them from afar off and his heart was vain of their coming. He shouted: "Iss, I speak true religion. The Big Man commanded me to build this altar. He said: 'Make you Calvary so tall that you can discern even the littlest in Sion returning from his adultery. Horrible is this sin in the Capel.'"

The company arrived at the foot of the altar. Lloyd Schoolin spoke: "Why for you lose your breath?"

"Better lose my breath than my soul," Pedr answered. "More costly than all the sheep on the moor is your soul."

Bern-Davydd stepped forward: "Clap up. Pilferer you are. Like the old boy who was crucified. Give back to Schoolin bach his one sovereign."

"Wild words with no meaning he speaks," said Pedr. "What use has Pedr for yellow money?"

"Creatures," Bern-Davydd cried, "know you all that Lloyd Schoolin possessed a yellow sovereign. Then, well-well. Old Pedr must suffer for his thieving. Fetch Morgan Polis we will. Come you down, now, the frog."

Lloyd Schoolin ascended to the top of the altar and he hurled Pedr upon the floor of the moor. "Don't let him run away, boys," cried Lloyd.

The company herded Pedr to the Schoolhouse, and they tied together his feet and put him in the Schoolin's henloft. Pedr whined to the Big Man to overturn the walls of the loft; he whined until his voice was become a whisper; and he wept that God had taken the part of the sinners of Sion. He asked for bread and water; none gave him any. In the early morning of the third day Lloyd removed the trapdoor and said: "Take off your snout, bad bird of the Fiery Pool."

Pedr moved slowly. On the way to Calvary he licked up the dew that was on the grass, and from the foot of Calvary he gazed at the faces of the sheep around him, and communed with himself: "Well-well, now, animals bach do not go into the Palace." He cast off his garments and sought the face of God, saying: "Like a porker I came, Big Man bach, and like a porker I return. Dear me, now, Jesus nice, don't you send me a White Shirt."

VIII
SONS OF THEIR FATHER

THE CHILDREN OF Essec were gathered at their father's bed; their names – from first to last, naming even John, the child of his wanton days – were John, Amos, Daniel, Ruth.

John was high and thin, with a narrow eye and yellow skin, a niggardly beard and sparing lips; and the Big Man, in whose sight he was without favour, had branded his forehead with a black mole. His years were fifty.

Amos was a little man; his countenance was mild and his eye unclouded, and his chin was covered by a red beard which waved beyond the opening of his waistcoat. The days of Amos were forty-three years.

Hairy also was Daniel, his stature was neither high nor little, and he was squint-eyed. The years of Daniel were forty.

Ruth was a child of her father's weakness. Her years were twenty-five; her way was showy and her mind was vainglorious.

These, counting John, were the children of Essec Penparc; Penparc the farm which is on the slope of the hill that rises from Avon Bern to the moor, and all the land thereto – which is both arable and pasture – is good and fat.

Now concerning Amos. The man was endowed with wisdom and much religious understanding. He spoke to his brothers and sister: "There's nice that we are all here to see father bach flying."

His words did not please Daniel: "The male foolish, why for you speak like a lean old pig? Have you better sense of the Evangel. Crossing the Jordan father bach is, and his Sabbath boots, dear me, will they not be dry when he meets the White Jesus bach on the Shore?"

John sat on a stool. "Awkward is this happening, boys bach," he said. "Killed the old meadow I did yesterday. Ripe will the hay bach be on the day of the funeral."

"Ach y fi," cried Amos. "Spout like an infidel you do. A corpse is before all things, John bach. How speech you now if we sing a weepful hymn, and I make a large prayer in a loud tone?"

John rose from his stool, and spoke in a small voice: "Ask a question bach will I before his old boots touch the water"; and he thrust his face close to Essec's face and said: "Very worthless is the meadow, little father. Poor bad is the hay crop. Say you then that the meadow is my inheritance."

"Woe me," said Amos. "Why for you make me savage, man? Don't you, boy bach, worship the meadow."

"Crafty old mare," John replied, "is this a light thing for me to lose the meadow?"

Then Daniel opened his lips: "White will be your Shirt, man, in the Palace if you speech this to me: 'To you, Dan, I give Dinas, all but the moorland. See you, I must deal even with Ruth, for is she not of my loins? So we give the moor to her.'"

No answer came from Essec, wherefore Amos turned upon his brothers and sister and sang in a religious fashion. These are the words which he sang:

"Boys, boys, where is your faith? Awful you are to mock the Big Man at this hour. See you not Gabriel bach beckoning his finger at my father Essec? And prattle you do of wickedness. What is the Big One saying: 'Essec Penparc, you have done fairish. Come, now, to wear a White Shirt. This parting must not sadden you; is not Amos your photograph?'"

"Stallion of a sow," said John, "how you preach preaches when there is business need settling?" He moved closer to the bed. "Father, waggle your tongue."

"Iss, indeed, father bach," spoke Daniel, "as you mouth: Dinas you give to me."

"For sure, I must have word," said John. "An awful stealer is Amos. You give the meadow to me. Iss-iss."

"Loutish sparrow, if I was not to have Dinas why you did not say so before now?" said Daniel. "Manure patent I scattered on the land. Costly that was. Go you and ask Shop Co-operative in Castellybryn. But you give me Dinas, don't you? And when persons speak to your son: 'A good farm you've got, Daniel. How came you by her?' I shall answer: 'This is my father's blessing.'"

Amos addressed the big Man: "Wise Farmer, be not over-harsh with the iobs. Daniel and John think more of manure patent and meadows than of White Shirts."

Ruth passed between her brothers and the bed: "Father, then, give you the old moor to Daniel and Dinas to me. A place bach very nice for sheep is the moor. Dear to goodness, Matilda Daniel manages Dinas wastefully. Ruffle you not the Big Man by holding Dinas from me."

This angered Daniel and he spat upon Ruth's face; and he said to her: "What for you mess about where there's no mess to be, you black white cat?"

Ruth moved to the window and peered through the close darkness; and she saw a light on the floor and heard sounds; and when she had understood the meaning of that which she saw and heard, she spoke to her people:

"Great is the moaning outside, little folk. The spirit Hound is at the gate of the close. Look you, too, the Corpse candle." She removed her skirt and bodice, and she drew over her the funeral gar-garments which she had put on Essec's bed. She also wept, as the manner is, saying: "Father bach is very dead."

Having done these things, she said to her brother Amos: "Sharpen you the edge of the razor and heat water will I, for many will come soon quickly to gaze on the carcase."

Daniel put his hand under the clothes which covered Essec, and there was not any warmth left in his father's body; and he said: "Act like a bad black you have."

John turned to Amos: "An orphan bach am I. Don't you pilfer the meadow, now, Amos."

When Amos had shaved the face of Essec his father and placed his father's hands on the Book of Words, he knelt on his knees and closed his eyes and prayed. He told the Lord how he had wrestled with religious strength against the unbelief of his brothers and sister, and sought mercy that he had not prevailed; and to the Lord he also said that he was more religious than any in the house of his father.

IX
A MIGHTY MAN IN SION

WHERE THE TRAMPING road goes out into the Cardigan road you will see Tycornel. This is the house in which lived Ellen Pugh, who is buried in the field that is between it and the road. Ellen had not known any man before her age was twenty-six, although her great thighs, and her soft, flaxen hair, and big breasts – of which much could be seen because her garments were sewn ill together – excited the desires of many men. If in the hayfields a vicious lover foxed her, or if on the way home from Sion one waited for her in a secret place, she always prevailed against her adversary: the woman was strong and she was proud of her chastity. She fastened her door at nights, and drew a curtain over the window of the room in which she slept. Though men came and looked narrowly, none saw her without her garments.

One night Lias Carpenter stood outside Tycornel and cried in a loud voice: "Ellen, now indeed to goodness, your cows are in my bit of field."

Having clothed herself, Ellen opened the door. "Sorry am I, Lias Carpenter," she said. "Fetch the creatures will I in a hurry."

"Wench fach, don't you trouble overmuch. Male very reasonable am I."

"Iss, for sure. Tarry you a while, Lias, and drink a small cup of tea."

"No, dear me; iss, dear me," Lias answered. "Very good is tea bach."

Ellen removed the crust of coal and clay which was over the fire and put sticks in its place; and as they two ate and drank, Lias spoke: "Big is Matti Rhys Shop."

"So I see, Lias. Four children has Rhys. Every year Matti is big."

"A large one bach is Rhys for system. Children you ought to have, Ellen."

"Sober me, Lias Carpenter, why for you talk like that? Shut your lips, man."

"Large the families Boys Israel had. Tell words will I." Lias thanked the Big Man for that which he had eaten and drunk, and turned to go away. He said: "Bring you home your cow on the morrow. Jasto, not safe is the bar on your door."

"How you speak?"

"See you, female fach." Lias went outside. On the flagstone he told Ellen to close the door and bar it. The woman did so, and then Lias gathered together all his power and broke the bar.

Ellen was astonished: "Glad am I that you displayed me this weakness."

After Lias had put a new bar on the door, Ellen spoke to many people in this wise: "Neighbour very kind is Lias Carpenter. And there's harmless he is. Trust him I can with me."

The people answered her: "Trust not your male before you win him."

For five nights Lias drove Ellen's two cows into his field, and on four nights he stood without Tycornel, crying: "Wild are your creatures. In Lias's field they are. Goodbye, now." The fifth night he entered the room wherein Ellen slept, and he awoke her: "There you are! Told you I have in plenty. Come I have in the rain to tell this, and my trousers are wet. Touch you them with your hand fach."

"Well-well, Lias Carpenter," said Ellen.

"Speech how shall I dry them, woman fach very fair?"

"Talk you like that."

"Harmless is my spirit," said Lias. "Close your eyes. Ach, put your old private garments from my sight. Not religious that they pollute my eyes." Thereafter Lias frequented Tycornel, whither he arrived and quitted in darkness and away from the common track.

It came to be that Ellen said to him: "Boy bach, wed me you must."

"Speak will I to mam," answered Lias.

"Iss, do you in a haste."

"Indeed, speak will I. Fair day for now."

Ellen was troubled that Lias did not come any more to Tycornel and she connived that men and women should not discover her plight. She drew in her clothes, and as her size increased she eased them; her contrivings did not withhold her state. Folk said to her "Many handfuls of gravel have been thrown at your window. Whisper the name of the thrower."

Before she delivered her child she pleaded in the hearing of Lias's mother Shanni: "Woman fach without wickedness, make your son verify his pledge."

Old Shanni answered angrily: "Ho, ho! And is the bitch saying that Lias is the father?"

"Don't laugh, foolish Shanni. Serious is affairs."

Old Shanni tightened her lips and called to her Lias, who had kept himself close: "The strumpet of Tycornel says you are the father."

Lias opened his mouth, and a frothy spittle fell therefrom upon his beard. "Dear me," he said. "Bad lies you talk."

Unable to contain herself, Old Shanni spoke savagely: "Go you off, you concubine of the big belly."

Ellen bare a child and she named him Lias, and after she was recovered fury possessed her: she cried, as a peevish child cries, on the Tramping road, and in Shop Rhys, and at the Gates of Sion that Lias Carpenter was the father of her infant; and she would not be quieted, nor charge anyone else.

Her shoutings vexed Lias. He shammed innocence before the Respected Bern-Davydd, to whom he sacrificed a hen, and whose counsel he craved, lamenting how Ellen proclaimed this and that to his discredit. Bern-Davydd ordered the woman to the Seiet, and caused her to stand in the Big Seat in the face of the congregation; and after the wily men of the High Places had laboured to prove her with questions, he lifted his voice: "Name the man bach you tempted."

Truly Ellen answered.

"Sparrow of a pig, no-no. A liar you are. Very religious is Lias. Is he not in the Big Seat?"

"He was bad with me," Ellen said. "Didn't I put his trousers rib before the fire?"

Bern-Davydd interrupted her: "Shut your head, you bull. Senseless you are to talk trousers rib in the Big One's Capel. Your bastard is by old Satan. Congregation, here's a sin. Shaking and redding you are. Good that I am here, for am I not the Big Man's son? Lias Carpenter, say things."

These are the words of Lias Carpenter: "Dear people, stop you a time bach. Shedding tears am I, and they are salter than the weepings of Mishtress Lot. Evil was she, but boy very pious was Lot. Changed was she into a rock of salt; a rock bigger than the biggest in Shop Rhys. Let out tears will I this minute." Lias wept. "Look you on the marks of the tears on my whiskers. So-ho, the wench says: 'Lias Carpenter was naughty with me.' No, dear me. Am I not full of the White Jesus bach? A carpenter was the Big Jesus. He made coffins. Iss, people bach, religious is the male that makes coffins. Wise is the Respected. He said: 'The Bad Man is the father of your hog.' Does Ellen not bolt her door and her window? Thick is the bolt I put on her door. Can a man walk through a door? Can a perished corpse come out of a screwed down coffin? Boys evil there are who die and wish to live. Sinners they are. That is why we use big screws, little folk. Ask you their length in Shop Rhys. Like would I now to hear the Respected report."

Bern-Davydd acquainted God with the perfidy of Ellen Pugh, and God gave him terrible words with which to scourge the woman.

Ellen was broken out of the Seiet. Even so, her rage against Lias did not abate one jot. She invented means to bring misery upon him: she pretended goodwill and helped him to gather in his wheat and at the finish of the day went into his bed, but Lias would not sin with her. She stole secretly into his house and placed stones in the midst of Shanni's butter, insomuch that this became a proverb in the marketplace of Castellybryn: "Say how much your butter weighs without the stones?" She opened the gates of his fields and set his cattle astray, and she maimed his horse to its death. All these acts and more she did in her hatred against Lias Carpenter.

At the age of forty-five Ellen was as one whose years are seventy: her teeth were fallen out, there were sores on her legs – sores which dampened and stiffened her stockings – her hair was grey and clotted with many sorts of residue. She grew weary, and complained that the day was too long and the night too short. A hope came over her that Death was near, and a fear that she would be buried in the same burial ground as Lias Carpenter. She said to her son Lias Small: "Perishing is your mam, boy bach. When I am dead, don't you say to anyone: 'Come and put a White Shirt on mam.' Dig you a grave in the field, and bind me with sacks, and bury me there in the darkness. Hap I shall hear the Trumpet before Capel Sion. Goodness everybody, there's things I shall speech to the Big Man about Lias."

Ellen died and her son bound her with sacks and buried her in the field. Then he became frightened and he ran this way and that way in his confusion and he told everyone whom he met that which his mother had said to him and that which he had done. Lias Carpenter heard his sayings and went to the owner of the field and bought it; and he built a hedge on all sides of it so that none should trespass in it. Moreover he raised a pulpit of wood near to the place under which Ellen lies; for he too shall be buried in the field, and at the first sound of the Trumpet he will arise and go up into the pulpit and he will warn the Big Man that Ellen Pugh was without a name in Sion.

X

A SACRIFICE UNTO SION

TY'R PECHADUR – meaning the House of the Sinner – is at the end of the narrow way which is between the new and the old burial grounds of Capel Sion. It is named thus because Griffi Wernddu died in it and because the Bad Man came up to it and hid in the belly of a pig, in that form imagining that he would go in and defile Sion. The Bad Man moreover left his marks on Griffi's body.

Griffi lived to an old age, and though he was full of religion and obeyed the pulpit in all its commands, he offended awfully in his death; and as is the custom with those whose souls go down into the Fiery Pool, Griffi's body was not enclosed in a White Shirt and it was buried in the land which is at the forehead of the Capel, and upon which the congregation perform privily before entering Sion.

At the time of his prime Griffi was one of esteem and conse-quence. He had a place in the Big Seat and he held the office of the Teller of Things. He dwelt in Wernddu, the farm whose fields are on this side and that side of Avon Bern. He prospered by the diligence of his wife Betti, who laboured until the members of her body were without feeling. In the mean season Betti bore eight children, and of the eight one grew into manhood, and he was named Dewi; and it was that at the age of sixty-five a pain caused Betti's wasted breasts to swell, and the woman died. Whereat Griffi endured much misery, for he had a great regard for the gains of his wife, and he sighed that he could not get another woman to serve as Betti had served. After a year was over and he had put away his grief, a man came to him saying: "Now-now, Griffi Wernddu, give you me the portion bach, dear me, of the mortgage that is due." Griffi and his son Dewi and his woman servant drove two milching cows and a heifer to the fair.

The next year he was constrained to sell more of his cattle, and the money which he got for them was not enough to pay all the people to whom he was bound. His straits was sounded abroad; people pointed their fingers at him and nodded their heads, speaking in this sort: "An old rotten one is the black. Not a brown penny has he now that Betti is perished."

Presently Dewi reached an age of knowledge, and when he looked about him and considered how the land was barren from long neglect and how the fewness of his father's cattle was a byword, he was very concerned, and spoke to Griffi his father: "Having gone very bad is the farm fach. Say a talk."

"Trying me is the Big Man," Griffi answered. "Loss indeed, Dewi, was the going of your mam fach."

"A person listless you are, little father," said Dewi. "Why for you don't work? Look you at me. Do I not toil every one minute? Must we hire a manservant?"

"Sense that will be," replied Griffi. "An old man bach am I."

"There's a large wage he will want."

"Iss-iss. Much white money he will ask. Buy trousers rib will I to-morrow for to work with you."

But Griffi did not help his son to till the land; he wore his cloth garments every day, and on such occasions as he was not in faraway Capels hearing the Word preached, he discussed the meaning of this and that religious problem on the Tramping way or in Shop Rhys.

For a long spell Dewi laboured as though his father was dead. But one night he said to him: "Carting in potatoes am I the next day. Come you and help."

"No, now," Griffi answered. "Are there not big preachings in Castellybryn? Going am I there."

"Dull you are," said Dewi. "Move you, now."

"Does not the little Evangel come before all? Not right that the father be a servant to his son."

As soon as night was over, Dewi said to his father: "Lift, man, and come and cart potatoes."

Griffi closed his eyes: "A rascal of a son have I got, Big Man."

Dewi went out, and he returned with a thickish stick with which he punished his father, and screeched Griffi never so loud, Dewi did not stop until he was weary; and his enmity against his father never lessened.

Now as Wernddu became fruitful and profitable, Griffi grew feeble and spiritless. If he rested in his labour, Dewi would kick him and speak spitefully to him. In the heat of a certain day, Griffi uttered a doleful cry and fell between the handles of the plough he was guiding, and he remained in that wise until the hour of the midday meal. Dewi came into the field and took away the rope upon which Griffi had fallen and unharnessed the horses, saying: "A bad boy is the fool; iss-iss. Animals bach, hungry you are." He took the horses into the stable, and on the way thereto he gave them water to drink and in the stable he served them generously of food; when he had eaten, he returned to the field and awakened Griffi into consciousness.

That day Dewi communed with himself: "Six years have I tilled Wernddu, and there's hard have I worked. And my earnings are not half a hundred sovereigns. Lazy mule is old father. God, indeed, now, why did you take mam first? A grand labourer was the female." Immediately he went into the room in which Griffi was, and said: "Father, go away from Wernddu must you."

"What is you saying?" replied Griffi. "All right am I."

"No-no, man. Heavy you drag on the farm. Make you to go off."

Griffi entreated: "Let you me remain here in my house, boy nice."

Dewi did not listen to his father; he rented the straw-thatched, one-room cottage which is now named Ty'r Pechadur, and he put in it a bed, a table, and a chair, and he planned to give Griffi sixpence a week and a little milk and cheese. But Griffi would not leave his bed, and he complained that the sickness which had felled him was still upon him. Dewi took him down from his bed, and put him in a cart and drove him to the cottage.

So it was that Griffi was cheapened in the eyes of Sion: none bid him to pray or to bear testimony in the Seiet; and to another was given his place in the Big Seat and also his office. The congregation scorned his plight, and Bern-Davydd cried out his name because of the poorness of his sacrifices. He became ashamed of the harm which was done against him; and he prayed that Bern-Davydd and God would show forgiveness unto him. Neither attended him. He prayed for a manna of two sovereigns. He said: "Large Lord, do this for me and all the yellow sovereigns bach shall I not give them to your son in Sion? Be with the Preacher nice. Amen." He prayed that prayer on five occasions, and each night he opened his ears so that he could hear God's footsteps and he closed his eyes because it is spoken in Sion that only the religious can see the face of God.

As God did not take any heed, he went in the night to Wernddu; at the gate of the close he paused. "Big Man bach," he said, "many prizes have I asked you, and you gave me nothing. A son of Capel Sion am I. Did I not Tell the Things? Come with me now. Keep by me. An angry boy is Dewi. Be with your son in Sion. Amen. Amen. And Amen, Big Man."

He drew his clogs from his feet and walked up to the pigsty and lifted therefrom a pig; and the pig he hid in his bed; and he praised the Lord very much.

Wherefore Griffi cloaked his gladness, and ceased to pray. By and by a horrid fear seized him: he had nothing with which to feed the pig. He contrived means and shifts; he locked the door so that his son, who was bemoaning the loss of the pig, should not enter his house, and he crept into outhouses and gardens and stole potatoes and carrots. But the man's heart was faint, and he gathered little; yet all that he had he gave to the pig, and the animal did not thrive.

There came a day when he closed his door and tried to go upon his bed, and he could not; the hour of his travail was come: the sickness of Death was on him, and all his strength was departing from him.

Three days passed, and Bertha Daviss came to his door, crying: "Griffi, now, indeed to goodness, pulling potatoes am I the next to-morrow. Come you and help a poor woman."

Bertha cried out several times before she heard sounds within the house, and made her afraid; and she ran hard into the Meeting for Prayer. "People, people," she said, "the Bad Man and his satans are in Griffi's abode."

The congregation moved as one man and hurried thither. They also shouted outside the door, and as none answered from within the stalwart men pushed with much force and broke a way through the door, and the pig fled thereby into the old burial ground. When Bern-Davydd saw this, he spoke in a big voice: "Run, you blockheads. The swine is going into Sion."

The congregation did in accordance with Bern-Davydd's word, and the fleetest among them was Dewi, who grasped the pig at the door of the Capel, and lifted it in his arms, saying: "This is my prodigal pig bach which was lost and found again. There's thin he is, dear me."

After they had viewed the pig, the people went into the house; and some of them raised Griffi from the floor and put him on his bed; and they all beheld the wounds which were in his body.

XI
THE DELIVERER

ALTHOUGH JOB STALLION was instructive in prayer and joyous in song, he was without esteem in Sion. The place of his abode was Cwmcoed, which is on the land that rises from the other side of Avon Bern, and the name of his mother was Peggi; and they two had a maidservant whose name was Hetti. Job searched among the women of Sion and among the women who frequented the fairs of Castellybryn for a wife who would free Cwmcoed from the mortgage which Amos Penparc held upon it; of the daughters of Sion and of the women who went to the fairs none would wed him because all had knowledge of his state. This also was spoken: "Hetti is breaking her hire. Thick is the wench by Job."

One day Amos came to Cwmcoed. Peggi saw him from a long way off, and she shouted to Job: "The old scamp Amos is after yellow money."

Job joined Amos in the lower field, and he was moved to say to him: "Like the happy Apostle, indeed, man, who walked with the White Jesus, I feel."

Amos gave no understanding to Job's words, and he said: "Speech I have for you, Job Cwmcoed."

"Well-well, now?"

"Wounded I am to speak. That smallish bit of money. Job, dear me, repay you the yellow ones."

"Not meaning you was; say you now," said Job.

"Why for you speak lightly?" answered Amos. "In mouthing does not my neck get dumb?"

"Ho, ho. Thus, indeed, then."

"Old money must I have, Job."

"Give money I would if I had him."

Job cried to his mother Peggi: "Serious, old mam, Amos Penparc wants his money."

There was much earth in the crevices of Peggi's face, and her body was bent from service on the land, and she shivered when she heard the words of her son: she seemed like a sapless tree which harbours every refuse that the wind blows.

"Solemn is this," she said. "Sell the stallion bach you must, Job."

"Religious you speak, little woman," answered Amos. "Does not the Book of Words say to us to pay our debts? There's bad would I be to speak to Daniel Auctions: 'Go, sell Cwmcoed'."

Job was enraged with his mother that she had borrowed money from Amos Penparc, and he told her that her life was a heavy load upon him. Peggi was too old to weep: she made yowling sounds.

In the evening she craved Job's forgiveness. "Woe to us," she moaned, "that we are on top of Amos's old finger."

Job was aroused out of his sluggishness, for he was in narrow straits, and he meditated: he planned to go to the Market of Carmarthen, where he was a stranger, to seek a wife among the women who gathered there. Hence the sixth day, which was the Day of the Market, he made himself to appear gay: he clothed himself grandly in cloth garments, and he covered his crooked legs with cloth leggings; he combed the hairs which were on his cheeks, and he put a bowler hat on his head.

Then he ordered Peggi to saddle for him the pony and to bring the animal to the gate of the close. Peggi did accordingly; and when he was on the pony, she spoke: "Don't you now, heart bach, be tempted by a bad girl on account of her looks. Beware of fair women. Go court a wench whose nice purse is as big as a fatted bullock's belly."

"Spout like a bull you do," Job answered. "What is the matter with the root of your tongue? Why don't you clap up the backhead of your neck?"

"Close you must, Job bach," Peggi persisted. "Shall the cow Amos take away our farm?"

"Hie off," said Job, "and suck your toes."

Job rode away; and on his journey he fixed his mind: if Cwmcoed were taken from him he would be called a fool in Sion. Sell the stallion bach he could, but the cost would not pay all of that which was borrowed from Amos. Did not the red mackerel say: "Glad am I to lend you money, Peggi fach?" Dear me to goodness, what a black the old snail was. Tight, dear me, was Amos. Good, now, if Jesus bach smote him with a flame of fire like He did the Unitarian infidel in Castellybryn. Job also explained to the Lord how that the borrower should be the payer; how that Cwmcoed and all the land thereto, and all that was in the land and on it was his if Peggi took wing.

Outside Shop Llewellyn Shones he magnified his holdings in the presence of Enoch Boncath – a man of twenty-five heads of cattle and one hundred and twenty acres of good land – and after he had boasted for a long while he said: "Misther Enoch bach, say you what now if I looked merry on your female daughter Ann."

Misther Enoch was unfamiliar with Troedfawr and the land and the people in that neighbourhood, and inasmuch as Ann was stricken by the disease king's evil, he replied: "Open your throat to the damsel. Go now to the House of the Market and say to her: 'Talked have I to your father.'

Job came down to Ann, who was sitting on the ground; her legs were crossed, as a tailor crosses his legs, and her outer skirt, which was of black cloth, was drawn up so that she sat on her scarlet flannel petticoat; and before her was a tub of butter. Her right cheek was marked by the malady which was upon it, and around her neck she had a band of calico which was wet with the moisture that drained from her wound.

"In private I will counsel in your ears, Ann Boncath," said Job.

"Comic one you are, man," replied Ann. "Speak for what."

A toothless woman, who sat by Ann, spoke: "Very quiet the stable of the Red Cow is, indeed to goodness."

A dealer drove his testing scoop into Ann's butter, and he bought it. Ann rose, and as she passed away the toothless woman said: "Give the wench one of rocks Mari."

Job took Ann up to Mari Rocks, and he purchased for her a sweet-meat, and as the custom is, Ann did likewise for him; and the people around and about observed that which was done, and remarked: "Boy bach, great shall be your courting this night." To Ann they said: "Very catching now is king's evil."

They two walked out of the town and into a field. Presently Job said: "I will go and make a league with Misther Enoch your father."

And Job passed into the town to make a league with Ann's father, and after he had said many pleasing words, he said this of himself: "Wonderful is my religious fame in Sion. Honouring your girl am I to take her into Cwmcoed."

"Glad is your speech, boy bach," replied Misther Enoch. "Yet now just not no nor yea can I say. Come will I and spy over Cwmcoed."

At the middle of the next day Job came home and he told his mother everything. Peggi's mind cherished vengeance; she gazed across the valley to the parcel of trees in the midst of which is Penparc; and her sight tried to pierce the mist which covered the Hills of Boncath, from whence was to come her deliverer. She petted Job, for she knew that he had established his right to Ann; and she served him with broth and pancakes; and Job, having eaten his fill, slept. She designed to go to Penparc and say slyly to Amos: "Here, male bach, is your ugly money. Take you the small sum: hap you want him largely. Sorry I am you are so poor. May he give you a yellow heart. Horrible were the words of the Big Man about the Calf of Gold."

She designed further: on the coming of Ann she would go into Shop Rhys and buy soap, and she would clean herself with soap and water and rest from toil. She would name herself headwoman of Cwmcoed – the mistress would say to Ann: "Do you this" and "Do you that," and Ann should be as a servant in her house.

In the folly of her gladness, she showed malice against Hetti: "Move your heavy body, you large trollop."

"Peggi, dear me," said Hetti. "This one minute, do I not suffer pains then? An old child bach is about to come."

The words incensed Peggi: "Sober me, why for you did not say you were thick? Run you home, you nasty harlot. Is not Enoch Boncath and his daughter Ann coming on the sixth day to view the land?"

Hetti excited her spirit: "And say to Ann Boncath will I that this is Job's child."

Old Peggi was dispirited that moment, and she feared for her schemes. She tore out from a hedge two slight twigs, which she coupled together, and with which she punished the servant woman. Hetti fell forward, whereupon Peggi raised the maid's garments and beat the flesh of her body.

At first Hetti made a great noise, then she became silent, and Peggi knew that there was no more spite left in her.

Her body grievous, Hetti walked out and up into the loft which is over the stable and gave birth to a child. The afternoon of the second day she returned to the living house, and she looked oddly as she held up her infant before Peggi's eyes. "Peggi, the female fach," she said, "who is this that has come from Edom?"

Thuswise Peggi was consoled that the Lord had not deserted her. She said to herself: "Very tidy is the little Big One to His children bach." To Hetti she said: "Mad you are, the wicked animal. Go you away."

Hetti bared her bosom and pressed her child's head against her breast; and in that fashion she walked along the Roman road and over the heather to her mother's house – which is on the top of the hill that goes down into Morfa. She did not harass either Peggi or Job afterwards.

On the sixth day Enoch Boncath arrived to search out the land and to establish by questions that Job had not exalted anything; and to all his questions Peggi devised deceitful answers; and Job moreover showed him fat pasture that was beyond the boundary of Cwmcoed, saying: "Iss-iss, that is our land, boy bach." But Enoch was cunning and he inquired of strangers; one answered him: "Job, dear me, is a tardy old sow. All, look you, his land is wasted. And does not Peggi owe much yellow money to Amos Penparc?" Enoch pondered the sayings which were told him for ten days, and then he came to Cwmcoed to speak abusively. Having delivered his speech, he said: "Send Sheremia Polis Boncath I will after you."

Job strengthened his spirit and feigned anger. He said: "Male out of his head are you; and there's a scamp."

"Iss, for sure me," said Peggi. "Behave you do like a colt."

"Count the days you can," said Job, "that Ann will display her thickness."

"Out of sin has come the disease of your wench," cried Peggi. "Did not Job wash his body when he came home?"

"Dark is your talk," Enoch said. "The damsel fach is all right."

Enoch journeyed home, and on his way he thought on the sayings of Peggi and Job; and every day he said this to Ann: "How you was?"

"So and so are things with me, father bach," Ann at last answered him.

"Well-well, bad black is Job Stallion." Enoch came out of his house; he told no one of the place whither he was bound, and so that none could imagine his purpose he walked through field paths and lanes. He reached Cwmcoed at the milking hour.

"Come have I yet again," he said.

"My boy bach has turned his mind," said Peggi, "and he is throwing gravel indeed at the window of a fine ladi. Male frolicsome is Job."

"Say you like that," said Enoch. "Sad am I that I spoke quickly to you. Ann wants to wed Job."

"What for does Job need an unhealthy wench? No-no, man. Go home, Enoch Boncath: busy am I preparing for the marriage."

"Woman fach," Enoch said, "be not hard now. Ten yellow sovereigns and six cheeses will Ann bring with her."

"Empty is your voice," said Peggi.

"And there's a one she is for making butter."

"Goodbye, Enoch Boncath, and goodbye to your thick Ann."

"Fifteen yellow sovereigns will Ann bring with her, and a waggon-load of hay."

"Three hundred is the number of yellow sovereigns that Job will get with his wench," said Peggi.

Job entered the milk shed; his mother said to him: "Old Enoch Boncath is here. There's a big pleader he is, for sure me."

"Waggle your tongue," said Job.

"One very high you are in Sion, Job Cwmcoed," said Enoch. "Be you religious and take Ann my female daughter."

Job and Peggi goaded Enoch so that he became as one who is drunk; and it came to be that Ann settled in Cwmcoed and her marriage dowry was two hundred sovereigns, a cow in calf and a heifer, a plough, a bed, and a load of hay; and when she was settled she saw that the land was indeed barren by neglect and that rust was on many of the implements. As the time of the birth of her child came near, her malady grew worse and it ruffled her temper, and she hated Peggi and Job because of their guile.

"Get up, you hare of the Fiery Pool," she cried to Peggi in the darkness before the dawn.

"No-no. The dawn is not grey yet," Peggi whimpered.

Ann removed the cloths which covered her mother-in-law and dragged her down from the bed.

The old woman rose from the ground: "Headwoman am I. Go out and labour, you concubine."

Ann gave no mind to Peggi's words; but she reviled Job because of her.

"A rotten old woman is my mam," said Job.

Howsoever Peggi contrived, she did not become the headwoman of Cwmcoed; she was made to labour in the outhouses and on the land, to sleep on a straw mattress in the straw loft; she never changed her garments, and earth and dung fastened to the material thereof like sun-dried clay. She clung to her life through the summer and the autumn of the year; in the winter she lost it and was buried in the burial ground of Capel Sion; and in her agony there was none to comfort her or to minister unto her. Job also Ann forced to labour all the light hours; and though he murmured against her tyranny, he obeyed her in all things. In his perplexity he plotted mischief against her, and plotted he never so constant, Ann would not abate any of the rigour of her dealings with him. He was as a hired man in Sion, and without dignity in his house. His state vexed him greatly. He brooded over Ann's harshness, and he planned a scheme by which he would win an advantage over his wife: he dampened the feather bed on which she slept. Having done that, he said: "I shall not lie with you any more, for your disease stinks."

He dampened the bed many times, and the day came that Ann went up to her bed to be delivered of her third child. She became very sick, and died. Job put a White Shirt on her, and at her open grave he wept and said: "Big Man, forgive the woman: fond of old money she was and very nasty she was to mam fach." Then he prayed a prayer which he had rehearsed, and raised his singing voice in a holy hymn.

XII
JUDGES

AFTER ESSEC PENPARC was buried John Tyhen would not give over the meadow to his brother Amos, although that it was a portion of Amos's inheritance from Essec, and although that in the face of the congregation Amos stood at his father's grave and proclaimed that his patrimony was just. Of that John took no heed, for the man's manners were harmful: he performed service on his land on the Sabbath, and his Sabbath garments were not respectful unto Sion, and he coveted temporal possessions. So it was that Amos came down to the Shepherd's Abode, and spoke to the Respected Bern-Davydd:

"Do him forgive me, little Preacher. Don't him think me insulting or irreligious that I come here in my worldly clothes. Heavy is my spirit – heavier than the grand stone I'm putting at the head of my father's grave. And to whom shall I go for counsel bach if not to the Respected?"

"Amos, dear me," said Bern-Davydd, "the Judge of Sion is right-eous, man."

"Sanctimonious he is, religious one," said Amos.

"Put your backhead on a stool, Amos son of Essec, and shake your tongue."

"Indeed, down is my spirit, little man. Is not John plotting against me because my father gave me the meadow?"

"Amos. Amos. Not speaking serious you are."

"Iss. Disheartening are the words John shouts of me."

"Don't be vexed, Amos the one good. Very harshly will the Man of Terror deal with John."

"Bad now that a brother reviles a boy bach like me."

Bern-Davydd sang: "Where's the old profit though the black gains the meadow and loses his White Shirt? Not his knife, nor his trousers. Not his wheelbarrow, nor his clogs. But his soul, male bach. Terrible Man, smite the blackguard John. Speech to me, little boy, the rent of the meadow."

"Well-well, small is the money, for sure. Angry would the Big Man be if I mouthed nay to my father blessing."

"Wise you are, boy. Go forth will I and hold inquisition over the sow and lord it over him. Explain the bigness of the meadow."

"Of acres two; of worry a cartload."

"Loss awful to Capel Sion when Essec flew. Go you to his place in the Big Seat."

"Holy that will be."

"Ask the Great Judge will I how to deal with John," said Bern-Davydd. "The meadow is worth two sovereigns a year, shall I spout?"

"No-no, Respected Preacher bach."

"Is he worth a sovereign and half a sovereign?"

"No-no, man. No, indeed."

"Don't be jokeful, Amos. Speak."

"One small yellow sovereign, Preacher nice."

"Ho-ho. A slip of a miser is John. And he is a worse old thief than his cat. Look you, we will tell against him."

Bern-Davydd called on his wife Sara, and he said to her: "Bring you my preaching coat, and my cuffs, and fasten you my collar about my neck, and put on my feet the elastic boots."

Then he said to Amos: "Come, Amos Essec. Let us go up to the mountain."

When they reached the top of the moor, Bern-Davydd made an utterance. This is that which he uttered: "Not saintly enough are you to come into the Big Man's presence. Tarry you here while I climb the mound to hold forth." Before he departed, he emptied his mouth of its spittle and laid the pellet of tobacco that was in his mouth on a stone: and so with a clean mouth he reported to God. Presently he came down, and he replaced the tobacco, and took the india-rubber cuffs from off his wrists and the collar from off his neck.

"Amos the dirty son of Essec," he said, "sin has come from your throat. Ach y fi, the awful swine. Scrape her with a shovel. Why for you say that the meadow is worth a yellow sovereign?"

"Little Respected," Amos answered, "I said that in my littleness. Wishful was I to hide John's avarice. Forgive him his servant."

"Shut your head. Thus saith the Big Man: 'Costly is the meadow, Bern bach, at a yellow sovereign.'"

"And like that the Big Man?"

"Thus saith the Large Farmer: 'See you, photograph, that Amos keeps the meadow, for is he not Essec's blessing to him?'"

"Amen, Bern-Davydd bach religious."

"The Man of Vengeance saith: ' Tell you Amos that you will rent the meadow from him for one half a yellow sovereign to be paid on the day of the Hiring Fair. Of the grass that grows there the pony that carries you about and about to preach preaches shall eat."

"Don't he say I" cried Amos, and he doubled up his beard and put the end thereof into his mouth. He mumbled: "Do I not need the meadow for my cows? Is he not the best grazing land hereabout? Be him sensible, boy religious of the pulpit."

Thereat Bern-Davydd pitched his voice: "Will you be as evil as John? Will you dispute with the Big Man?" He also appointed a set time, saying: "Such and such a day I shall take God's pony into the meadow. Hie you away and order John."

Amos said yea, because the close friendship between Bern-Davydd and the Big Man awed him. It was that in the dimness of the day he entered the field in which John and John's wife Martha were toiling, and he said: "Very messy is things after the old rain, little people."

John looked at his brother: "Why for you say extraordinary?"

"A mess, too, is life without the Palace of White Shirts," Amos replied. "Longish were the prayers I made this day."

"Talk a plain talk, Amos," said John.

"Rented the field bach have I to Bern-Davydd."

"Dear glory me, for why you act so strangely?"

"Was I not thinking of you, my brother, and of you, my sister?" answered Amos. "Grieved am I that you labour so hardly."

"Old man nasty you are to rent what is not yours."

"Hold your words, John bach," said Amos. "What does the Apostle say about kicking against the pricks? And did I not speak over the grave of father Essec that the meadow was mine?"

John remembered: by the sweat of his limbs he kept profitable the twenty acres of gorse land attached to Tyhen; he tilled and digged and drained, and his body was become crooked and the roots of his beard were caked with some of the earth that had enabled him to gather much wealth, even seventy sovereigns. He struck Amos.

"Meek am I in my religion," said Amos. "Above all the men on the face of the earth, I am the most humble." He turned upon his brother his cheek.

That night John set a clamp to the gate of his meadow so that no one could enter the field; and as he came back to Tyhen, he saw his cat eating the herring that remained from the midday meal.

"You wasteful daughter of a robin," he cried to his wife Martha. "There's bad you are. Why did you not hide the fish? Was he not as large as my leg? He would make the next day's meal also."

He went out and caught the cat and brought it into the house; and he called up to him Martha and his two children, and he laid the animal on the table and in their sight he killed it. He divided the carcase into two, and one piece he nailed in the door of Penparc, and one piece he nailed in the door of the Shepherd's Abode.

XIII
A KEEPER OF THE DOORS

ON A MORNING Leisa Llain addressed Michael her husband: "Near perishing, woe me, am I."

Michael answered: "What, old ox, is the matter with you to disturb my sleep? Odd talk you make through the backhead of your neck."

"Serious is my speech, little Michael," said Leisa. "Over laboured am I. Be you a boy bach nice, and clean the outhouses of filth."

Michael settled his countenance and reproved Leisa. Then he wailed: "Well-well, iss; well-well, no. A weak dear one have I been since I came to your bed. My mam used to make words: 'Lustful wench is Leisa Llain. Temptful is the wench in her bed, son bach of my heart.'" Michael turned his back upon Leisa and slept.

At the middle of the day his wife came up on his bed in all her garments, and she shrieked because of the pain that tormented her, and she complained that she would not recover of her sickness. Before the light of the day was spent, Michael awoke.

"An old woman cruel you are," he said. "If I was not feeble, one in the bone of your cheek I would give you straight."

"There's hurts in me" Leisa moaned. She displaced the shawls that were over her bodice, and the shawls that were under her bodice, and she beat her hands upon her breast.

"The Angel of the White Shirt is very near, female," said Michael.

"Wishful am I, man, that he was in me," said Leisa.

Michael came down from his bed and went to Shop Tailor – which is between the Garden of Eden and the School House – and Shonni Tailor said to him: "What is your errand, shall I say?"

"Why for you squander time, little man?" Michael replied.

84

"Solemn to have a corpse in your little house."

"Provoke me you do," said Shonni Tailor. "Mouth plain in my hearing."

"Flying is Leisa, indeed me, Shonni. Is not her feet in the Jordan already?"

"Bad jasto, now!" said Shonni. "Act you religious, and ask me to pray on the Night of Wailing."

Michael admonished Shonni: "Shonni, indeed, wasteful speecher you are. Look you, make at once in a haste respectable clothes for to bury Leisa in. Very black must they be, for wet will be my weeping. See here, put a flap fach on the trousers."

When Michael arrived home he put water in a cauldron, which he hung in the chimney over the fire, and he spoke to Leisa: "Making old water hot am I to wash you, female. Clean shall your perished corpse be on the Night of Wailing. Say a prayer will I now for you. Merciful will the Big Husband be that you are the woman of Michael Llain."

After he had prayed, he visited the places where the hens had their nests, and gathered together all the eggs, even the addled eggs which are left to entice the hens to lay; and he put all these eggs, and also those which had been collected, in a basket and took them to Shop Rhys, and the value of them was the price he paid for a White Shirt of the Dead.

Then Michael lay by the side of his wife.

Now the man was lazy from his youth up. He slept near to the end of everyday, except the day of the Sabbath. Then he arose early to go and take charge of the Doors of Sion. Thus he was become very fat. The labour of the six acres of land which are with Llain was performed by Leisa, whose temper was aroused because of the man's indolence. She voiced spiteful sayings against him on the Tramping road and in Shop Rhys: how his worth was less than the worth of an ass, how his bones were without marrow, how constant toil had blighted her fertility. With all, Michael had a name in Sion: he made monthly sacrifices of a white-hearted cabbage, or a sackful of potatoes, or a weight of butter to the Ruler of the Pulpit; and this was a proverb in the district: "Prayer bach very eloquent is Michael Llain."

At the end of a set period Leisa's pains were decreased, and she fulfilled divers labours in and about her house. She weighed her husband's sluggishness, whereon her wrath against him was increased. She exclaimed at the side of his bed: "Come out, you putrid cow. Why for you are like a sow?" and she took her clog from her left foot and struck his head with the heel of it.

"Don't you vex me, the accursed Leisa," said Michael. "What for you hit my little face? Saying things am I about your old corpse to the Big Man."

"Clap your lips, you swine of a toad," said Leisa. "By sloth you were conceived. Ach y fi, eighteen years old was I when I married you, and for five years I have not had minutes to clean my legs."

Michael repeated her words and told of her act to the Seiet of the Congregation, and he grieved that the woman's heart was turned apart from religion, and he said: "There's struggle will I with the Bad Man, people bach, when he comes up from Fiery Pool to fetch her."

He chose a portion of the burial ground beneath which Leisa should be buried, saying: "Tell you, will I, boys Capel Sion, when I hear the old Spirit Hounds." He also pleaded with the Judge of Sion not to withhold from Leisa the Palace of White Shirts.

The spring of the year passed, and the hurts of her affliction were come back upon Leisa. But she continued to trim the land which gave her little and robbed her of herself. She was grown revengeful against her husband: in the mornings she took away the clothes from off his bed until not one remained over him.

"Lift your bald head, you frog," she reviled him.

Michael was unmindful.

Leisa urged him to go into the fields of her neighbours, but he did not change his habit in any manner, and he stayed on his bed unto the cool of the evenings.

One Sabbath Shonni Tailor said to him: "Indeed to goodness, Michael bach, boast did you that Leisa's clogs were in the Jordan. Nice and long was the prayer I worded for the Night of Wailing. A bad blackguard you are to tell a lie, the man."

Michael was confused in the face of Shonni; had he not said: "Is not her feet in the Jordan already?"

"Shonni bach nice," he answered, "every day I watch for the Angel of the White Shirts. Weep I will when he draws nigh to Llain."

The Angel came presently. Leisa was labouring in a man's wheat-field. In the strong heat of the day she yelled: "Boys bach, hurts are in me," and she fell upon the ground. The people who were working encompassed her. The wife of the owner of the wheat corrected them: "Go you off, persons bach. Much has to be done yet." She dipped an apron in the water of the ditch that is in the field, and spread it on Leisa's forehead; and she hid Leisa's face from the heat of the sun with straw. In the dusk of the day Shonni Tailor raised Leisa from the floor of the field and carried her easily to Llain, and he said to Michael: "Religious glory is awaiting you, man bach. Is not the Angel of the White Shirts on his way to your abode?"

"Off, then, now," said Michael, "and voice that Michael Llain will wrestle with the Bad Man."

Michael drew off Leisa's garments and shawls and washed the body of her, and he put on her the White Shirt of the Dead; and he prepared much provision. Moreover he took a box and made a hole through the lid of it, and he set it on the window-sill by Leisa's bed. At last weariness overcame him and he went and rested in the cowhouse.

The great people of Sion came into Llain, and also small people were come with tin pitchers to carry water from Big Pistil which is against Llain, and the house was full from the end of the parlour to the fireplace; the praying men prayed and the singing men and women sang, and the many who departed to milk their cows returned and stayed in the house until the middle of the day, when Leisa died.

After all had eaten of the provision, even of the victuals which they had brought in honour of the dead, Shonni Tailor came into the cowhouse and awakened Michael: "Grease your boots, Michael, now, and wear your respectable black clothes, and come in and say: 'Shonni Tailor will pray last on the Night of Woe.' Rise, you boy bach nice; Leisa is in the Jordan."

Michael answered: "Don't say! There's wet will be my weeping when I wake."

XIV
THE ACTS OF DAN

DAN SON OF SHAN – a servant in Pentremawr, which is against the shores of Morfa – on a day said to his master: "Not wise that I labour for you. A photograph bach am I of the Big Man. How talk, then, if I say: 'I break my hire'?"

He put his clothes and his clogs in a wooden box, and he carried the box to Groesfordd, which was the abode of his mother Shan and which is at the foot of the hilly road that goes up to the Moor. He assumed he was above all the religious men in Capel Sion, and in the Seiet he rose and exclaimed: "Boys bach, a photograph of Big Man am I."

The Respected Davydd Bern-Davydd denied him, saying: "The fool is lame in the foot: old club is at the bottom of his leg, and light is the weight of his sense. Brawling evil is the iob. Shan fach, very grieved you are for your idiot. People, hear you Shan say now: 'Indeed, iss, Religious Respected.'"

Shan adored Dan. Her mind was elated that God had ceased His anger against her bastard son, and she prayed within her that the number of blessings He would heap upon Dan would be as the number of stones which marred her field. She muttered: "Murmuring, dear congregation, is always the boy bach to the One in the sky. Large joy he makes of his religion."

"Serious to goodness, off is your temper," Bern-Davydd said. "Lunatic is Dan. Boys Capel Sion, laugh provokingly at Dan Groesfordd. Know you all that I am the Big Man's photograph."

The praying men – the first praying men who were in the Big Seat – laughed and answered as with one mouth: "Words very well he speeches, Respected." The lesser praying men – they whose seats were on the floor of Sion – did likewise.

Howsoever the people mocked and chided him, none was able to entreat Dan to humble himself or to give over his false argument. He stood in the public places and proclaimed that he was the Son of God, and he prophesied that he would prevail above Sion, that he was the chosen Ruler of the Pulpit.

One day he took a bucket into his mother's field and made a tinkling noise upon it, and he cried: "Shoot! Shoot!" Thus he enticed up to him Shan's fattening pig. He seized the pig and carried it to the Garden of Eden. On the way thither he uttered with a great voice: "Sinners Capel Sion, come you, children bach and gaze you on what I do for the White Jesus nice. Awful is the religious dirt in your bellies." He put the pig on the floor of the Garden and killed it. Then he discoursed to the people: "Mountains of bad evil there is, boys. Did not the Big Ruler say to me: 'Now, now, Dan Groesfordd, picture of me you are, man bach. Hie off, and slay Shan's pig in my name!'" Dan Removed the pig to Groesfordd and Shan poured boiling water over it and scraped the hairs from off the skin, and when she had separated the carcase into small pieces, Dan said to her: "Go now the next day and sell the pieces bach to the people. If one says to you: 'Not wanting the flesh of pig do I' speak like this: 'Buy now, for sure. Is not this the swine that perished in the Big Man's name?'"

Shan obeyed the order of her son Dan, and she did not turn her face until she had utterly sold the pig, even the entrails, and when she returned she said to Dan: "Love bach of my heart, take you the yellow gold and white silver." She spread three shawls on the floor and rested upon them.

For two days Dan hid from the people, and he would not eat or drink anything. He came forth from his hiding place and lamented at the Gates of Sion: "Old mam fooled me to sell the corpse of the Big Man's pig. Stinging is my spirit. Ugly are the sovereigns and shillings she gave me. Accursed mam have I. And has not the Big One said: 'Dan bach, Jesus is on my right hand, and you are on my left hand'?"

As he was speaking a stranger woman, who was very large, stopped the horse that was between the shafts of her cart, and spoke to Dan these words: "What does the boy bach say?"

"Woman from where you are?" Dan answered.

"Ho, ho, the mishtress of Blaenpant am I."

"Puzzling you are," said Dan. "Where shall I say is Blaenpant?"

"O, well-well. In Conwil."

"Enlarge your mouth and tell the name of you and your man. There's sly you are to keep secrets."

"Is not my name Sali Blaenpant? Gone is the husband to the Palace of White Shirts."

"Dear me," said Dan. "Dear me. Abide do I with the Big Man. Not anything concerns me but Him." Then sang Dan Groesfordd: "Sali Blaenpant, is not the Big Man the landlord of all the fields? Even the land under the old potatoes He owns. Good He is to ones religious and bad to unbelievers. He did say to me: 'Dan bach, don't you now let an old razor touch the hairs of your face, because I will make you a photograph of the White Jesus bach.' A great pig I sacrificed and my Satan of Mam sold the saintly corpse. What for you say to that?"

"Serious sin," Sali the stranger woman answered; "give you a suckling pig will I."

"Stout, Sali Blaenpant, the pig was," said Dan. "To the Big Man you give a stout little pig."

Sali addressed her horse: "Gee, old mare fach. Goodbye, boy nice, and goodbye again"; and she departed believing. She spoke of that which she had seen and heard, saying: "The second Jesus is Dan Groesfordd." She sent to Dan a letter, in which she wrote that he was greater than all the rulers.

Dan journeyed to Blaenpant.

"How you was then?" he said to Sali.

"Very good, thanks be to you, religious boy."

"Much land you have here," said Dan.

"One hundred acres but ten acres," said Sali.

"Well and well," said Dan. "An old bother is a mortgage."

"Iss, boy bach. But there's no mortgage on Blaenpant."

"Happy you are in your offences," said Dan. "What will Blaenpant profit you in the Palace of White Shirts? Give did I all to the Big Man. Speechify religion will I now. This is what the Angel said to me the first night: 'Grand for you to preach preaches in a Capel.'"

"Wise was the Angel," said Sali.

"Poor am I in silver and gold," said Dan, "and rich in religion. How say you to a Capel Sink? White will be your Shirt."

Sali Blaenpant gave Dan three sovereigns and a fat pig, and the pig he sold to Sam Warts, Castellybryn, and the money he got for it, and also the money he had had for the flesh of the pig which was sacrificed and the three sovereigns he put under the mattress of his bed.

On the eve of the Sabbath he said to the tale-bearers of the district: "Jesus bach is inside me. Preach preaches will I on the first day in the void before the workshop of Lias Carpenter. Carpenter bach very handy was Jesus."

The tale-bearers cried this to Bern-Davydd, whereof Bern-Davydd was uneasy, and he visited the houses of the men who had the oversight of the congregation.

"Fools you are," he said to them. "The cow Dan Groesfordd makes mischief in the Capel. Horrible, then. Abominable is the man. Don't be calm, old donkeys. Displeased will the Big Man be if this comes to pass. Your horses will rot and a plague of worms will eat your sheep. Lightning will burn your bellies and crops. And I, dear me, will be called to play the harp fach. What will you do without me?"

The men of the Big Seat took each other's counsel, and they conspired to do Dan hurt; they sent the lesser of the praying men to Groesfordd to stone him. Dan heard the noise of their footsteps and went softly into a place of concealment. Before the morning light he came abroad, and having eaten and put on him his black garments, he moved to the void place which is before the workshop of Lias Carpenter; and as he spoke Sali Blaenpant stepped downward from her cart and stood by him. Some passed on their way to Sion, and were refreshed exceedingly with the music of his eloquence; they said: "Preacher bach not very bad is Dan Shan."

Dan preached for many Sabbaths, and the music of his eloquence gave religious delight to numerous persons; and every Sabbath Sali stayed by him. His name came to be greater than the name of Bern-Davydd, although Bern-Davydd accounted ill of him to God and counselled God to blast his body. His ownings increased: he had a milching cow and a heifer, two pigs, three sheep, and many hens; and he hired a field besides the field which was marred with stones.

Bern-Davydd essayed to subdue him. He rehearsed wrathful words that he would relate to the assembly that gathered in the void place, but when he beheld all the people that Dan had stolen from Sion, his indignation was so great that he could not speak.

He turned away and walked to Capel Sion, and he said to the

congregation: "Foul old blacks are you to allow the mule to be more than the Big Man's son."

A certain high man in the Big Seat ceased chewing his beard, and said: "Wo, now, Religious Respected, not right that he speaks so of us, his children bach."

"Dear me to goodness," answered Bern-Davydd, "go off, then, and pelt the male ram with your fists."

The certain high man said: "Good, too, that will be. How now if the young youths will do this for the Big Man's son? Take in your hands knobby batons."

"Close your eyes, young youths, and the Big Man will say sayings in my ear," said Bern-Davydd. In a little time he said: "Like this the Large Judge: 'Bern bach, array you the youths of Sion and send them out to whallop the frog Dan Groesfordd.'"

Nine sons of Sion took Dan down from his bed, and they carried him to the pond which is in the close of Penparc, and they placed him on the brim of the mess, crying: "Go inside, the man. Why for you do not go, I shouldn't be surprised!"

Because Dan hesitated, they urged him with the prongs of hay forks, and when he came out of the messy water they took his clothes from his body and drove him home; at the gate of the close three of the young youths raised him from the ground and carried him into the house, and as they put him on his bed, they beheld that Sali Blaenpant and Shan were there also.

Now Bern-Davydd had seen from a secret place all this which was done to Dan, and it was so that he waited the return of the young youths in the way of the gate of the Shepherd's Abode.

"Fair day, porkers bach," he said. "How was affairs?"

"Fair day," answered the youths. "How was he?"

Then one said: "Sali Blaenpant lies with Dan."

"Porkers awful!" said Bern-Davydd. "Mad is the shift of your tongues."

"Truth we speak, Respected," said the one who had spoken. "In bed she is with him."

Bern-Davydd was anxious; he spoke to himself: "The hog will grow strong on Sali's riches. Hap she will build for him Capel Sink, and rob Sion still more. Go will I and look him in the face."

He came to Groesfordd. "How you was, religious one?" he said to Dan.

"Mouth of your spirit?" Dan asked.

"Big is the little mistake I made about you. Great is my think for the son of Shan."

"Glad am I to listen to such and such," said Dan.

"Iss-iss, the man. Speak you the day bach of the wedding to me."

"Well, now," said Dan.

"Riches you will inherit, Dan bach nice. There's useful yellow sovereigns are."

"The earth is the Big Man's, Bern-Davydd," said Dan. "Selling Blaenpant is Sali fach, and the old money, will not I keep him in trust for the Big Man?"

"Daniel Groesfordd, make you a small prayer with clapped eyes, and I will listen for speeches from the White Jesus bach to bid you to Sion."

At the finish of Dan's prayer, Bern-Davydd said: "Amen, boy bach. Amen and Amen. The large Jesus says: 'Give Dan Groesfordd an important corner in the Big Seat.'"

About the time that Dan was installed in the Big Seat in Sion, Sali laboured, and she delivered a child before the time was ripe for its birth. Yet the woman was puffed up: as it was buried she cried out: "A photograph of the Big Man was the infant bach. Was he not Dan's son?"

Bern-Davydd said to Dan: "Boy, boy, awful is this you have done. Heavy must be your sacrifice unto Sion."

"Religious Respected," answered Dan, "deal him well by me. A bitch is the female."

"Say now your offer, Dan Groesfordd."

"Little have I of white silver and red pence," said Dan.

"Give you five yellow sovereigns in the collection plate on Sabbath Preacher," said Bern-Davydd.

"Nice little Respected Bern-Davydd, make you his talk less mean."

"Five hundred of pounds and half hundred you had for Blaenpant, for sure."

"Iss, dear me."

"Giving you are, Dan Groesfordd, to Him," said Bern-Davydd. "There will be joy in the Palace."

"Biggish was the price the rascal lawyer cost," said Dan. "There's old snails lawyers are."

"Important is your corner in the Big Seat, man."

"Say him a large yellow sovereign," said Dan. "Act him religious."

Bern-Davydd replied: "Put you the five yellow sovereigns in a parcel of paper, and form the words on the outside: 'This is for the beloved Ruler bach.' Go off up to the mountain will I then and tell the Big Man that you fell by an old female."

Dan obeyed Bern-Davydd, and he wept in the Seiet that women had caused him to meddle with them to his hurt, and he glorified God that his hand had been stayed from marrying Sali Blaenpant.

The next day he performed a second sacrifice: he brought out of Groesfordd the bed in which he had slept and an hour before the sun went down he burnt it because of its sin; and Shan he sent away to the House of the Poor, which is in Castellybryn, and he made Sali return to the district of her people, which is Conwil.

Afterwards there was peace on all sides of Sion.

XV
THE COMFORTER

THE RESPECTED Davydd Bern-Davydd lay on his face at the grave of his wife Sara, and while he wept he spoke: "Perished is your carcase, Mishtress fach. Three tens and three years we lived together. And what was you doing now, Sara fach? Playing the little Harp. Unhappy am I without you. Did I not show you how to serve the Big Husband? Great One, why for you drowned the candle that was in the Shepherd's Abode? In a haste you was, God bach: an hour or two and cross Avon Jordan would me and Sara together."

The congregation witnessed Bern-Davydd's solemn acting, and they said that the man's grief was heavy; and as eight of the strongest men in Capel Sion lifted the coffin and lowered it into the grave, every one that was of age bemoaned in an audible voice: "Having gone, indeed me, is the wife of our Respected."

After the grave was filled with earth and a mound was fashioned over it, Bern-Davydd commanded the people to go into the Capel; and he stepped briskly at the head of them, and they followed him in the manner of those that walk in procession. When all were gathered in Sion, Bern-Davydd went up into his pulpit and asked God by what violent means he could end his life. Then Bern-Davydd answered God: "All right you are, now, then, Big Man. So-so. Live you want me to keep your House respectable."

It fortuned that on the fifth Sabbath after Sara's burial Tim Deinol – Deinol is on the slope that goes down into Morfa – and his daughter Becca came into the neighbourhood to ask about the welfare of Josi Llandwr; Josi wished to wed Becca because he coveted Tim's belongings. They were arrived early in the day; and Tim put his horse in the stable which is against the House of the Capel, and he made himself familiar to Ben and Jane, the keepers thereof. These are the words with which Tim Deinol greeted Ben and Jane:

"How you was, boys bach?"

"How you was?" Ben answered.

"Give you the mare fach a feed of hay, now," said Tim.

Having done that task, Ben returned, and to him Tim said: "Journeyed to Capel Sion are we to hear the Evangel. From Morfa are we come to weep to the tune of the Respected. A deacon am I in Capel Saron. Do I not own Deinol, a farm, people bach, of three twenties and ten acres?"

As soon as Tim ceased his saying, Ben talked to Jane:

"Don't you stand there, old female, like a snake. Boil water at once in a hurry for to make little cups of tea. Sit they down in the best end of the house and tarry they till the moment they enter the Capel. Distant is the way from Morfa."

Jane served the strangers with tea and with the luxuries of the land: butter and white bread, sugar in lumps, and such cheese as shopkeepers sell; and she placed an apron over Becca's lap so that neither the tea nor the food, if any fell thereon, should soil Becca's black cashmere frock. Becca was neither young nor well favoured, and her forehead was marked with a blotch which was of the colour of a red cabbage.

In the course of his eating and drinking, Tim observed: "Jasto, now, cold are my feet."

Jane knelt down on her knees and took off his shoes and gave him a stool on which to rest his feet.

Then Ben withdrew and stood in the way of Sion's gate, and to the congregation which passed he spoke: "A rich man has come from Morfa to weep joy under the Respected."

"Speak you his name to us, man," the congregation urged. "There's close you are."

"His name is Tim and his farm is Deinol, and he has hundreds of acres of land, and water flows through every field, and the number of his servants is six. Wicked animals, why you wait? Go off away to your pews and be presentable."

In the fulness of time Bern-Davydd came into the House of the Capel and after he had drunk of tea and eaten of bread and butter he viewed Tim and Becca at a wide space, and he came up to them, saying: "Male and wife from where you are?"

Tim and Becca made such reverence as is due unto the Judge of Sion; and Tim also uncovered his head: 'A little old man am I to baldness. The wench is my daughter Becca."

"Ho-ho," said Bern-Davydd. "Tidy is the old wench."

"As he speaks, Religious Respected," said Tim.

"In a nice White Shirt is my Mishtress," said Bern-Davydd. "There's hard is my sorrow. Ask you of the congregation."

"Sounds of his weeping have we heard in Morfa," said Tim.

Bern-Davydd sang: "A grand woman was the Mishtress. She obeyed her husband and gave me two sons. The Big Man gives and the Big Man takes away. Blessed be the name of the Big Man."

"Amen, indeed. Amen. Amen," said Tim.

Bern-Davydd asked: "Say you the enterprise you have here?"

"Come are we to hear him expound," answered Tim.

"Dear me, iss. Too religious am I to spout about old business. Stop you, now, farms fach very nice in the land."

"That he says. Speak him the farm at the head of the old School?"

"Think you of Penparc?"

"No, no. High is the heap of manure in the close of her."

"Is she not Llandwr?"

"Iss, Llandwr. Farmer very strong is Josi Llandwr?" asked Tim.

"Indeed, so-so."

"Listen you, Becca," said Tim.

The woman said: "Ears have I got. What for you think? Beautiful are the Respected's words."

"Explain in a whisper why you demand about Josi?" said Bern-Davydd.

"Not this way; not that way. Heard have I of the boy."

"No odds, male bach."

"Iss-iss; no-no," said Tim. "Bulky is the purse his mother left him."

"The Psalmist bach says: 'Every man is a liar.'"

"Wisdom very neat," said Tim.

"Read you, dear me, the Book of Words. Now what the Psalmist mean? Every man. Not every ruler. The Big Man's son am I."

"One waggled his tongue to me in this way: 'Bulky is Josi's purse.'" said Tim.

Bern-Davydd answered Tim: "Purses cannot play the Harp. In the

Abode is the Mishtress's purse, and the Mishtress is playing the Harp. Boys bach, weep will I now badly."

In the middle of the day Tim and Becca supped broth at Llandwr, and Josi closed his beady eyes and said: "Make words will I to the Large One."

Tim did not regard Josi's prayer, at the finish of which he said: "Amen now indeed to goodness. Closing is the day. Do you now display your riches."

"Gladly would I do that for you," replied Josi, "but is not this the Sabbath: Jealous of His day is the Big Man. How speeched He about the breaking of him?"

"Religious your say," said Tim. "Many blessings has the Farmer given to you."

"Large, indeed, Tim Deinol. If this was an old weekday show you I would my cattle and crops."

"For sure, boy bach."

"And I would say: 'Lucky is the female I shall wed.' Youngish too am I: no razor has yet touched the down on my little face. Open my mouth I will now about religion. The Temple of Solomon was very pretty."

Tim considered with himself: "Much was the gold inside."

"Male bach, iss. Did not Queen Sheba give Solomon a lot? Rich was Solomon, and Queen gave him above one hundred and a half of yellow sovereigns."

"Prydderch in his *Explanations* says that half a hundred was the sum. I could not give Becca as much."

"Sorry am I that I threw gravel at the window of your wench fach," said Josi. "Well-well, grand bit of sermon this morning, man."

"How if Becca brings with her a sow?" said Tim. "Queen Sheba gave Solomon no pigs."

"Swine the little White Jesus called pigs. Some were possessed. Ach y fi!"

"The swine the Big Man spoke of," said Tim, "were not the pigs we know. Did He not speak in a parable?"

"Tim Deinol," said Josi, "wrangle you about the Word?" Josi looked up to God: "What do you think, now, Big Man! Tim Deinol denies the Word. Is he not a iob?" Thus saying he put on him his coat and his hat, and he feigned to go away.

His manner alarmed Tim, who laughed as frightened persons are accustomed to do. Tim said: "What is the matter with the boy bach? Swine are little pigs."

"And gold Queen Sheba gave Solomon," said Josi. "Many sovereigns."

"Iss-iss."

"The religious man gives all to his children."

"As you say," said Tim. "Leave you two will I now to say this and that." Therewith he went out and looked into Josi's barn, and he cast his gaze in search of implements which are employed on the land, and he studied the cattle which were in the fields of Llandwr; and he turned into the house. He said to Josi: "Wed you Becca fach. And all I have shall be yours." Immediately after he had spoken, he walked to the doorway, and on the threshold he spoke: "That's a handy machine separator you've got, Josi."

"No, man, no old separator have I," answered Josi. "Very useless she is."

"Save much cream she does," said Tim, "when you have many cows."

"The wench of a servant skims my cream," said Josi.

"Large is the labour, dear me. Well, farewell, then, Josi."

Now at the moment that Tim and his daughter were going away, Josi said: "Do not go in secret. Pass you do the Shepherd's Abode. Pained will Bern-Davydd's mind be if privily you off."

Even as Josi had desired, Tim stopped his mare and shouted: "Hello, here. Shall I say there are men in the Shepherd's Abode?"

"Come down, small people from Morfa," said Bern-Davydd. "Reasoning with the Big Man am I."

They two entered the Abode.

"Crafty boy is Josi Llandwr," said Tim.

"Mouth you wisely," said the preacher. "Base is the turk and miserable. Deceit is in his clay and his debts are as many as there are flowers in his land."

"Solemn serious, man nice! Say him more again."

"Low is the black. 'Denounce you Josi Llandwr in Sion, now, Bern,' said the Big Man to me. 'God bach,' I answered, 'without passion am I, indeed. And weary with sorrow.' The Big Man answered: 'Bern, for why you did not complain then, man? Send a wife to you I will in a hurry. But remember that bad is the herring of Llandwr. Has he not his eye on Becca Deinol? His old feet splay like the mouth of an avon.'"

"Thanks very great to you, religious Respected," said Tim. "We in Saron shall wail for a whole night for Mishtress Bern-Davydd."

Tim and Becca stayed over the night at the Shepherd's Abode, and in the morning they arose, Tim saying: "Large thanks, Respected. Off we go."

"Young is the day, dear me," answered Bern-Davydd. "Wait you a time bach."

So Tim and Becca remained until near twilight, and they rose again.

But Bern-Davydd said: "Don't you leave me now, then. Gone to the Palace has the Mishtress. Tarry you with me until the morning."

As the light of that day was darkening, Tim said: "Walking am I for the horse."

"A terrible one you was," cried Bern-Davydd. "Sit you down, you and the wench." He turned his face away, and he brought forth Sara's petticoat and frock. Of these he said: "Stoutish was the Mishtress. Take you off your affair, Becca fach, and clothe yourself."

Becca put on herself Sara's frock and petticoat, and she laughed, saying: "Well-well, a large woman I feel. How shall I say?"

Bern-Davydd replied: "A miracle bach the Big Father performed on Sara Abram." He laid Sara's Sabbath boots at Becca's feet, and he raised his voice: "Sit you down, Becca Tim Deinol, and draw the boots on your feet."

APPENDIX

'The Day of Judgment' and 'An Offender in Sion': Two post-*Capel Sion* stories

Of six Evans stories separately published in 1917, 'The Day of Judgment' and 'An Offender in Sion' were omitted from his third collection, *My Neighbours* (March 1920, though dated 1919), and were not printed during the author's lifetime. Closer in spirit to *Capel Sion* – 'The Day of Judgment' (*English Review*, February 1917) is a conscious sequel to 'Judges' – both are included in this appendix.

'An Offender in Sion' appeared in *Everyman*, 21 September 1917, the politico-literary weekly which, in its notice of the 'astonishingly powerful and extraordinarily dirty' *Portrait of the Artist as a Young Man* has spoken of Joyce as 'an Irish edition' of Caradoc Evans. The *Everyman* story once more takes up the case of a defenceless widow callously mistreated by a relative; Rachel knows that her brother-in-law Ianto, for all his religious posturing, intends to do her harm. The 'pig-wife from Shire Pembroke' faces an imposing alliance of farmer (one with 'a name above many in Capel Sion') and auctioneer, a man 'skilful in these things'; that is, in robbing the weak of 'all that was in the land and on the land'. Yet Rachel, gun at the ready, is not to be intimidated.

If *Everyman* wanted a reaction, it certainly got one, with a Swansea reader suggesting that Evans's 'atrocities' against his countrymen paralleled those of Houston Stewart Chamberlain, Wagner's English-born son-in-law, whose racial theories had led him to side with Germany in 1914-18 war. Evans's reply, elevated to the status of an article (*Everyman*, 2 November 1917), exemplifies his approach in such exchanges – which was to reaffirm his own position (often with a leavening of banter) rather than giving publicity to critics by carefully rebutting their points. Insisting that Nonconformity thrives on 'hypocrisy, brutality, lust', he alludes to religious leaders (wisely left unnamed though – it is implied – personally known to himself) who hate their sisters, cheat their brothers, despoil young girls, condone incest among their congregations and sometimes practise it themselves. The litany reaches a crescendo that strikes with the force of blasphemy. 'We are as Welsh Nonconformity has made us. Not until the last chapel is a cowhouse and the last black-coated worker of abomination is hanged shall we set forth on our march to the light.' At this an old adversary stirred. The Revd Arthur Sturdy, who had denounced *My People* from the pulpit, now spoke up on behalf of ordinary Welsh country folk and their superior morality. As for the high illegitimacy rates among them, he urged a proper perspective: 'A lustful peasant may be implicated in illegitimacy because in the innocence of his carnal heart he allows nature to take its course, but illigitimacy, undesirable as it is, is infinitely better than the scourge of prostitution and its attendant diseases and evils caused by the gilded town-dweller.' (9 November 1917).

The *Everyman* clash spilled over into the *Western Mail,* prompting one more frontal assault from Evans (15 November 1917), this in response to an outraged deacon from Llanfaches, site of the first Nonconformist church in Wales where his father and grandfather had been ministers,

> Sir – Mr G.N.W. Thomas is angry. He declares that I am not worthy to be either a Nonconformist of a churchman. I am a Nonconformist. But I am not a Welsh Nonconformist ...
>
> A Welsh nonconformist preacher does not hate intolerance; he thrives on it. Because he feigns teetotalism abroad and gets drunk within closed doors, he shuts down public houses; because he sees more gain for himself in Liberalism than Toryism, he makes his chapel a Liberal committee room; because he magnifies himself greater than his congregation, he has come to believe that he is greater than God. He has bullied the peasant people into putting up ugly chapels on hillsides and in valleys, and has set himself up in the pulpits thereof and proclaimed himself ruler of the people. He is the hangman of our liberties and the enemy of God.
>
> I am, &c., CARADOC EVANS
> 26 Thornton-road, East Sheen, Surrey.

THE DAY OF JUDGMENT

THE RESPECTED Bern-Davydd proclaimed against John Tyhen in Sion: "Boys, boys, there's an awful black for you. Half an old cat he pegged on my door the last night. Sober serious. Mishtress Bern-Davydd saw the filth. 'Keep him silent for a time bach,' she said, 'while I retch from my belly.' Words to the Big Man will I now sound."

This is Bern-Davydd's report: "A fulbert is John Tyhen, for sure me. Tempted was his father Essec by an old servant wench, and the iobess spat John. Easier for you to thread a camel with large horns and three humps through the eye of a stocking needle than for a bastard slip to pass into the Palace of White Shirts. Why isn't John like his half-brother Amos Penparc? Man very religious and wise is Amos, and much money he possesses. Go I did and say to Amos: 'Grass the pony that belongs to the photograph of the Big Man must have.' 'Take him the meadow that is in the hiring of John Tyhen,' answered Amos. And John was angry that Amos gave to the Large One. He slayed his cat, and one half of him he nailed on the door of the Shepherd's Abode and half on the door of Penparc. Mishtress Bern-Davydd is not flopped on her pew on this Sabbath of Bread and Wine, little people. Why for not? At the finish of her retch she lamented: 'Bern-Davydd, the Bad Man is closer than the Big Man. Not eat of the Flesh or drink of the Blood will I until the Bad One is beaten into stones as small as gravel.' What a speech, boys bach! This day the Judge said to me: 'Bern bach, have John Tyhen afflicted by the Seiet on the third night. I will set stiffness in his heart, and your messengers shall lay hands on the red frog. This would I do myself, but how can my white fingers play the Harp fach after touching the stinkard?'"

Bern-Davydd descended into the Big Seat and uncovered the bread and wine; the congregation ate and drank, and then he prayed:

"Well, Big King bach, glad are boys Sion that you have commanded them to bring John to the Seiet. Much will be the muster. If the bullock is obstinate send rats into his house, and vermin into the inside of his cattle, and rot his crops. Leave you the meadow. Good is the grass and very benefitful for the pony of your religious son. Amen, little White Jesus. Amen."

The people said: "Amen".

When all the congregation had heard of that which John had done against Bern-Davydd, the valiant men arose to do him hurt, and these are the chief men who gathered between the evening lights at the gate of the Garden of Eden: Davydd Bern-Davydd, Ben the Keeper of the House of the Capel, Lloyd Schoolin' who is the beginner of the singing in Sion, Abel Shones Poor Relief who is the most spiritual of all the praying men on the floor of Sion, Old Ianto of the Road who is the grave-digger, and Amos Penparc, whose riches in land and money are above those of any in the land. There were also many old women and young, and old men and young.

Now of they who presumed to fall upon Tyhen: Bern-Davydd and Abel Shones went into Sion to pray; Amos Penparc rested on the roadside because his clogs were new and hurtful, and he would have help from no one; moreover, when the procession neared Tyhen, some faltered, for they had understanding of the spirit of John.

Lloyd Schoolin' was the first to enter Tyhen. John was repairing the nose of his plough, and Martha his wife was suckling her infant and stirring the pigs' food which was heating in a cauldron over the peat and wood fire.

"Indeed, now, dear me," said Lloyd, "come you two at once to the Seiet."

"Well-well," John answered, "Come would I, but the plough bach I must use tomorrow."

"We don't use ploughs in the Palace, John," said Lloyd. "Why babble you like a blockhead?"

"Say you like that," replied John.

"Irreligious you are, man. Indeed to goodness, shift, and put on your trousers cloth."

John raised his face and these words came through his broken lips: "The cows are not milked and the pigs are hungry. Look after affairs must I. Large was the cost of the coffins of my two children who perished."

"Male Tyhen," cried Lloyd, "the Big Man calls you to account. A goat was you to sin against the Respected."

"Why then did he steal my meadow?"

"By the mouth of Bern-Davydd, the Man of Terror orders you to Sion", said Lloyd.

"Fair night, boys bach," John answered.

Martha counselled her husband: "Obey, John bach. Warn you did I against gathering in the hay on the Sabbath. Go, now, and take a nice hen fach to the Respected."

"Shut down your neck," John admonished his wife.

A woman of Sion pressed her yellow face close to the suckling infant, and as she spoke the loosened black tooth in her mouth trembled. "Is this your child, John bach Tyhen?" she cried. "Many have been with your hussy. Ach y fi, Shim Tinker is the father of the brat."

"Don't say," Martha pleaded. "No strange man has known me."

The men and women of Sion rounded John and Martha; and the man they seized and took into the close, and having fastened him with a rope to his cart, they brought forth the woman and her infant.

Lloyd Schoolin' cried with a loud voice: "This is Gomorrah. Children of wickedness must be cleansed."

"Iss-iss," the woman of Sion voiced.

"As dirty with smell they are as a hen loft," said Lloyd. "Wash the dung from their flesh."

The pond of Tyhen is at the foot of the close, and into it the rains bring much of the residue from the cowhouse and the stable and the pigsty; and the water is still water.

John saw that he was put to worse before Sion.

"Persons, don't now," he cried. "Come with you will I. Drop dead and blind, come will I."

The men unbound him and they drove him to the brim of the pond, and as he faltered one urged him with a hay fork. John walked through the pond; he was a high man and the water came to his knees. Martha's stature was little and the water lifted her garments as far as her thighs; Lloyd Schoolin' peered closely, and then opened his mouth, speaking in this sort: "Boys bach, look you. She is not husband-high to John. Wet she will be for Shim Tinker."

Thereafter John and Martha were taken to Capel Sion, and they were made to stand under the pulpit, which is in the eye of the congregation.

Amos Penparc rose in the Big Seat, and turned his face to the people, saying: "Little sons and daughters of the Big Man bach, true that John has made himself my enemy, but very forgiving am I to those who curse me. See you, here is the piece of turk-cat he nailed on my door. Still, I forgive the bull-calf. Am I not saintly and full of religion? The loutish rabbit sinned against the Big Man's son. There's merciful is the Respected that he didn't say to God: "John Tyhen is at my door. Kill him with an axe!" Remember you the old infidel who died in the Shire Pembroke? The Bad Man left the mark of his clog on his body. Deal you not too harshly with the bastard slip. Nor think the lighter of me for his sin. Have not the sayings of his iniquity made my ears tingle?"

Amos placed the carcase which was nailed in his door beside that which was nailed in the door of the Shepherd's Abode. "There is your cat, Son of Satan," he said. "Say you why you did this vile thing."

It was so that John's courage weakened, and he lied and charged Martha with the fault, and he also called her to bear witness of his guiltlessness; and Martha, who calmed her infant's cries with her breast, said: "Serious, my male knows nothing of the turk-cat. Go we will now. The cows are not milked, and a feeling of foreboding curdles my milk."

"Wicked spider," cried Lloyd Schoolin'. "The Fiery Pool is curdling your milk. Respected, whip them with prickly speeches."

"The night of yesterday," said Bern-Davydd, "the Big Man came to me in a White Shirt. 'Bern-Dafydd! Bern bach!' He called. 'Big Man,' I answered, 'your photograph listens.' Thus the Large One: 'I will perform against John Tyhen all and more than I have spoken to you concerning him. Of him and Martha and their children and their cattle will make an end. I will devour the robin's sovereigns and silver. Burning is my anger. Tell you the toad to make sacrifices unto Sion.'"

"Glad would I be to give," said John. "A large little cabbage I will bring him."

"Clap your mouth, fool", cried Bern-Davydd. "Why for you make messes when there was no mess to be?"

"Pilfer my meadow you did," John answered, and he did not try to discourage the fury that was rising within him, for his heart was mean and he was covetous of all things.

"John bach," said Martha, "obey you the voice."

"Why for must I toil for Bern-Davydd?" John replied. "Do I starve for him? My two children perished and fat was the pig I gave for their coffins. Ask you Lias Carpenter. Lias, speak, man."

Bern-Davydd closed his hearing with the tips of his fingers. "Chase them out," he commanded, "like Big Jesus did the swine, or hap the roof will fall on my religious head."

John and Martha were driven from Capel Sion. The valiant men and women followed them and stoned them to the door of Tyhen. That night, before the wicks were turned down in the lamps of the Temple, the children of Sion gloried that the Chapel was purged of sin; that they had done all that the Big Man had commanded them to do by the tongue of His son Bern-Davydd ...

Martha milked her cows and separated the cream from the milk and fed her pigs, and when her labour and the labour of John were ended, they two looked upon their infant, and behold it was dead; and the Bad Man had branded its forehead with the mark of a stone. John, humbled to rage, lifted his face and raised his voice: "Cruel you are to me, God bach. Wasting much am I in burying the perished. Turn you your think, dear me, and put back the life into the wench fach. Be with your son in Sion. Amen."

He waited for the performance of the miracle until the body stiffened. In the break of the day he sacrificed a lamb unto Sion.

AN OFFENDER IN SION

FOR HER STUBBORNNESS to her brother-in-law Ianto, who had a name above many in Capel Sion, the Big Man lamed Rachel, widow Enoch Coed, in her legs, and he branded her body with the prongs of pitching forks, so that at the judging his preachers shall remember her wickedness.

On a day Rachel spoke up against her brother-in-law, Ianto.

"Woman fach," Ianto answered her, "not very good are affairs. Do we have enough faith in the Large Farmer?"

Rachel replied that her brother-in-law's words were becoming.

"Glad would I be to let you stay in the small place," said Ianto. "Fertile is the land and worth many yellow sovereigns. Is not money a load on my soul? But the land belongs to the Big Man."

"Like a preach is your mouthing," said Rachel. "Grand for you to say in that way."

"Has He not talked: 'I am the landlord of the Palace of White Shirts and the earth'?"

Divining the meaning of Ianto's words, Rachel cried hastily: "Old thief you are, for sure. At his perishing did not your father give Coed to Enoch?"

Ianto observed Rachel: "There's colour, dear me, in your face."

"Fulbert very black you are," said the woman.

"Say fairly will I now," Ianto remarked. He laid his hands on Rachel's shoulders, and he spoke flatteringly and made false promises. He said this also: "Tidy, look you here, you are in your blood. Softening I am. Come you into the lower end and talk matters will we."

Rachel placed her trust carelessly in him; and it came to be that after Ianto had committed his sin he repented and he rebuked Rachel: "Awful, serpent, is this you have done."

Wherefore Rachel laughed, saying: "A baban bach I shall get and the name of his father I shall noise in Sion."

"Shut your throat, temptress Coed," Ianto commanded in his anger. "Tell tellings of you will I in the ears of the Big Man. Much will be my muster."

"Be you nice now," said Rachel, "and let me abide in the place bach."

Ianto lamented: "Ten over twenty was the age of Enoch when the Big Man struck him for wedding a pig-wife from Shire Pembroke."

At the side of his bed he reported to the Big Man: that a woman had sought to hurt him, that the woman was of a loose nature, that her hair was yellower than the flowers which marred his cornfields, that the middle of her body was pressed in a manner most abominable unto Sion. He told how that the twelve acres of Coed land were as a wilderness of gorse and heather, how that broken hedges divided the fields, and how that the walls of the cowhouse were crumbled. "Wifeless old boy am I," he said, "and there's an unsullied one. Barren was Rachel to Enoch. Keep you her barren, little Big Man."

In the morning he went to Coed. Rachel saw him when he was afar off, and she put on her a white apron and she puffed up her hair.

"How you was, female?" asked Ianto.

Rachel feigned pleasure. "Put yourself in a chair," she said.

"Here am I on small business."

"Certain sure me," replied Rachel. "Close the door will I."

"No-no, Rachel Enoch Coed. Heap of dung you are to flaunt your body before me."

"Deal you evenly now with your maid," Rachel pleaded. "Sorry am I to know your message."

"Sober serious is my inside."

"Wait you a time bach, and all right will the land be. For two years have I laboured alone. Since Enoch winged."

"Windy is your speeching. Weep do I as I gaze upon the soil. Account must I give to the Farmer in the Big Farm. Go you off."

But Rachel would not depart; and Ianto took counsel and was instructed how to seize Coed and all that was in the land and on the land. To Hews Auctions, who is skilful in these things, he said:

"Come you up, Hews bach, and make a writing of everything Rachel has. Charge nothing to your memory. Say you nothing. An old Pembroke pig is the wench. This is a whisper between us."

Before Rachel was aroused, Hews was counting her belongings. When he had performed a little of his task, Rachel came to him and proved him, and after she had received his answers, she ran to Ianto's house; and she pursued her brother-in-law to the door of the lower end; and she screamed as a woman in childbirth.

"Rachel, now, indeed to goodness," Ianto cried from within, "still your tongue. Did not my religious father rest here in his White Shirt?"

Rachel would not be soothed.

In a great fear, Ianto stepped through the way of the window. Rachel heard his going, whereat she followed him into the close.

"Don't you be savage, little woman," Ianto said. "Turn your mind. Speak civil will I this one minute."

"Son of hell on fire, why sent you Hews to spy my ownings?"

"Harsh you are. Boy pretty good is Hews. How says the Book of Advices: 'Judge that you are not judged'? Iss, indeed, you, Rachel fach. You. Not me. Not Hews. You."

"Tell him out."

"No sense is in your spite. My arm is spread not against you. No, drop dead and blind. The lawyer rascal has done this."

"You fondled me," Rachel shouted. "And am I not large? Stallion of a frisky frog you are."

These sayings distressed Ianto, for he did not know whose ears received them. "Jesabel," he said lowly, "shut your chin, or kick your belly will I."

"Why then send me off?"

"Disquiet you are. The last Sabbath the Respected said: 'Don't be greedy after old treasures, people bach.'"

Ianto knelt and closed his eyes, and he prayed in behalf of Rachel's sins; and as he prayed Rachel threw a spade at him, and the spade cut into his flesh.

Thereafter Ianto hoarded his vengeance; and at his ordering Hews Auctions came to sell all that was in and about Coed. Rachel was strifeful and stayed in the house, and she cried at a window: "I'll slay you, Hews bach."

Hews was attended by the people, some of whom mimicked his halting footsteps. One said: "Afraid you are of a hoyden."

Rachel cast a stone. It struck Hews; the man fell, rose again, and escaped swiftly.

"Boys, boys, is she stronger than Sion?" Ianto asked the assembly. "The little Big Man is on our side."

The people strengthened their force; and many lifted their voices: "Why for you not come out, whelp of an ass"; and they broke down the door. Beyond the threshold they beheld Rachel with a gun at her shoulder. They turned upon one another speedily, and each hid himself and none returned. All knew that Rachel had stored much violence in her bosom.

Ianto pondered: and he drove into one of Rachel's fields three yearling calves. Presently he arrived to view them, and, lo, one was missing.

"Hai, now," he cried. "Where is my calf bach?"

"Am I your shepherd?" Rachel answered.

"There's a cost are calves."

"I killed your calf."

Looking upwards, Ianto rebuked the Big Man: "What for you say to this? Put my calf I did in your keeping. Higher price was she than a sheep. "He roared his concern so loudly that his sound was heard beyond three fields.

Rachel would not cease her mischief. By day she guarded her house and by night she passed stealthily into her brother-in-law's land and maimed the cattle therein. It was so that Ianto watched for her comings, and at the dawn of a morning he came upon her; wherefore the woman, having knowledge of her danger, hasted into his barnyard and covered herself with straw. Ianto made a show of seeking her, but he did not go away from the barnyard. He summoned to him his manservant and his maidservant, to whom he said: "Untidy is the yard. Clear the old straw we will into the stable. Get you pitchforks."

Then they three drove their pitchforks into the straw.

THE EDITOR

Formerly a Lecturer in Bibliography at Aberystwyth, John Harris has edited numerous works by Caradoc Evans, and is an authority on Anglo-Welsh literary history. Most recently he has published *Goronwy Rees* (University of Wales Press) and an edition of Rees's autobiographical writings.

Also introduced by John Harris:
Caradoc Evans *My People*

Other Seren Classics:
Dannie Abse *There Was A Young Man from Cardiff*
Rhys Davies *Print of a Hare's Foot*
Margiad Evans *The Old and the Young*
Siân James *A Small Country*
Christopher Meredith *Shifts*
Gwyn Thomas *Selected Short Stories*